A Wordsmith

Angela Craddock

ISBN: 9798363472862

Author Biography

Angela Craddock lives in the North East of England with her partner Anton and their fox terrier, Teddy. She greatly enjoys books, foreign travel and cooking as well as spending time with family and friends. Her love of reading has been a lifelong passion along with a burning desire to be a writer. She founded The Buddies Book Club in 2013, bringing together a collection of friends who share a love of reading. All of those original members are still enthusiastic participants. She views reading as a way of broadening the mind; stories are gifts to us from authors who share observations from their unique perspectives. She finds writing to be a cathartic process of self-expression and an interesting forum that entertains her readers. After working as a qualified nurse in the NHS for 35 years she has gained a wealth of experience and feels privileged to have helped her patients through every stage of life's bittersweet journey.

She is educated to degree level having achieved a Bachelor of Arts degree in Nursing Practice and a Postgraduate Certificate in Infection Prevention.

Following her retirement in 2020 she is delighted to have published her first book, 'Rookery Heights' and has written an extensive collection of short stories. Her best ideas spring to mind on breezy walks along the coastal path between Whitley Bay and Tynemouth.

She is living her best life and has stopped waiting for Friday!

Email: angelacraddock22@gmail.com

Twitter: AngelaCraddoc12

Instagram: craddock.angela

Facebook:/angela.craddock.5

Dedication

This book is dedicated to my precious partner Anton Davidson who has stood by me through good and bad, happy and sad times. Thank you making me laugh when you are not even trying to be funny! All my love to you.

Special Acknowledgements:

To Gladys Smith, my wonderful Mam. Thank you for everything, for your enthusiasm for my stories and loving me as you do. You mean the world to me.

To Eve Smith, the kindest and best Aunty who I'm very lucky to have.

To Julie King, my dear cousin and dedicated fan of my stories, thank you for always supporting me.

To all the members of my Buddies Book Club : Patricia Taws, Diane Rutledge, Lisa Wood, Sandra Sandy, Stephanie Hannant, Judith Pike and Veronica Holland. Thank you for your on-going support.

To Amanda Mills, my lovely friend for her thoughtful ways and for boosting my book sales! Thank you so much.

To Dawn Wilkinson, my friend whose most valuable input has helped to me to publish this, my second book. My thanks to you.

To Michelle Taylor, my friend who inspired me to write one of these stories. You are beautiful inside and out!

Contents

Distance

When everything you've dreamed of

Seems like it's just too awfully far,

And the whispered voice of doubt

Has been ingrained in who you are,

Do not curse the distance

For it provides the time to grow,

What would be the point of dreams

If you could reach them in one go?

~~e.h

The Wild Inside

You've been to this gate before to admire the delicate filigree structure, a representation of splendorous nature beyond. The design is mesmerising, the trees appear free flowing in the breeze, as if in denial of their rigid fixing. Birds which perch on the branches are gracefully spellbound there. You noticed the flowers and fauna soundlessly waving within the metalwork and reflected that the photograph did not do it justice. You looked through but you did not see. There is a subtle though vital difference.

On Autumn evenings like this the sun gives up its last rays and dusk sheds an atmospheric, haunting mist which allures some visitors and repels others. You have never ventured beyond the gate before, and you won't do so today. There is too much to explore and not enough time. I know you will prefer to return in Summer when nature gifts its greatest visual display and the lazy days buzz with busy insects. All year round this gate is a picture frame for a seasonally evolving landscape. Sometimes a red squirrel plays on the gate. His beady black eyes curiously stare through the mesh at those who study the intricate design. He is certainly not the prisoner he feigns to be! His tickly whiskers are laughing in irony that he has such a free and natural playground.

On the crumbling path you must be careful not to slip into the river, not that you will come to any great harm. The loose stones can easily steal your balance and rob your footing. Be mindful of overhanging branches and bushes that grow unruly and the gnarled roots protruding from the ground. Listen to the sharp crack of snapped twigs beneath your feet. At this spot the water is merely a constant trickle, gaining fortitude and momentum further downstream. Carefully cross the rickety, moss-covered bridge and notice how sticks and stones are dragged along with the flow, wending to an unknown destination. Now you are in the shade of a huge ancient tree; even in a downpour you would remain dry under this leafy canopy. Look up and see the shafts of sunlight beaming through the foliage. Have you ever known and appreciated such verdant shades? I'm taking you to a wildflower meadow, through a sea of bluebells and onwards to a carpet of random colour and beauty. Nature's haphazard display could not be made so perfectly imperfect by man. You have finally returned! Now is the time for you to open the gate and walk through. You have won your freedom. Your lifelong investment is both your gift and reward. No longer are you shackled to the walls of the work establishment or trapped by time constraints and obligations of employment. I am your *wild inside spirit,* indeed a sprite, a nymph unleashed! I will accompany you on the journey I described. Open your eyes to these pastures new, savour every little detail and fully nurture your senses. Run free in this country that ever flourishes on the wild side.

Pining for Green Therapy

Eleanor is owned by a rambunctious fox terrier called Barney. With wiry fur and bright appealing eyes he is a clever manipulator and is even better at getting himself into scrapes of all kinds. In the woods he explores in the thicket, chases small animals and recently got stuck down a rabbit hole. Despite his naughty tendencies Eleanor loves him and takes her everywhere she can. Today though, Barney must stay at home, left on duty to bark at passers-by, on important window sill lookout for his arch enemy, the postman. He is poised and ready for action and his whole body jumps to the beat of his bark.

Eleanor has had a hard time lately dealing with some life issues, but with the help of her cognitive therapist, Mrs Reynolds, she is feeling much more positive. It's her penultimate session today and she wants to discuss some ideas for a new venture that she hopes will have a 'feel good' factor.

Climbing the steps to the third floor office Eleanor was slightly out of breath but she just had enough time to gain her composure and wipe away some beads of perspiration. Mrs Reynolds opened the door and smilingly invited her in.

"Hi Eleanor, nice to see you again! How have you been since our last session?

"Well I must say I've been feeling much calmer and I have been practising the Eye Movement Desensitisation and Reprocessing technique we've been working on. I've been trying to slow down my thoughts with mindfulness meditation with some success but also some distractions. I want to talk to you about something specific. The other day I saw something that gave me a new idea of how I might be able to help myself. I was walking Barney, my dog, in the woods and I saw someone hugging a tree! Yes, right there, arms around the great big trunk, in a world of his own until Barney started ragging his trousers and jumping up! I was full of apologies because I knew he'd interrupted an intimate moment between man and nature," she said, whilst starting to chuckle. "Anyway, it started me thinking that I'd like to have a go, so what do you think? Eleanor studied the facial expression of her therapist, noting only an evolving smile before Mrs Reynolds replied, "Wrapping your arms around an arboreal friend, mindfulness in nature! Known as 'forest bathing,' the Japanese call it shinrin-yoku, believing it helps to connect all five senses with the environment. There's lots of evidence to suggest that tree hugging can improve mental clarity and well being, producing feelings of calmness and bonding", endorsed Mrs Reynolds. "Hospital patients who look out on trees have been found to require less painkillers and make a faster recovery than those who do not, so there must be something in it."

"Can you do it in a group then? I'd feel a bit vulnerable out in a forest on my own," stated Eleanor.

"Yes, they are called eco-psychology workshops, and I agree that you would be safer and better supported within a group setting. Also it's an enhanced experience with a course instructor who leads the session. I can put you in touch with someone if you like? I hope it will be the cleansing and enlightening experience you want it to be".

The old Volkswagen campervan pulled up into the woodland car park. The waiting group already guessed that their instructor had arrived, just as she jumped out and dramatically announced, "Hello ladies, I'm pleased to meet you all, I am Yoh...land...duh!

Eleanor waved and was first to step forward to introduce herself. Next was Jude, followed by Anna. The three ladies, guessing they were all fellow group participants, had spoken to each other prior to the flamboyant debut of Yolanda, who sported a floral-patterned headband, kaftan and orange sun shades. She re-positioned a thick, grey plait over her shoulder, smoothing and twisting it fondly as she spoke.

"Ladies, how are we? I hope you are excited and almost ready to get started! Firstly, I want to find a quiet spot where we can cluster before our ecological experience begins. I will set out the housekeeping, or *ground rules* as I prefer to call them and then we will each share our purpose with the group, starting with me!" Yolanda sprang like a wood nymph to the shade of a huge oak tree. Under its leafy covering she asked them to gather around. "Is everyone alright with sitting cross legged under these magnificent branches? Getting down there is fine but sometimes people struggle to get themselves back up!" she mused. The ladies all obediently sat as requested, in a small circle and listened to what was required of them.

Yolanda began, "I am here as your instructor. I want you to take a life changing journey into the woods that will recalibrate your natural energy fields and reconnect you to planet earth. I need you to make a commitment to Mother Nature that you will unlock the power of trees and appreciate the sanctity of this sacred space. No devices are allowed in order that you can fully enjoy the sensory elements of the forest. You will remain as quiet as possible, unless I ask you to speak. You will all slow right down, take long breaths into the abdomen. You will stop, stand and sniff". At this point Eleanor stifled her first uprisings of laughter. She was picturing Barney trying to obey commands.

"We will progress through the woods at an ultra-slow pace, observing every small detail that nature has to share with us. Do you all wish to continue?" Yolanda enquired.

No one dared to say no, so in unison they replied a fairly resounding, "Yes".

"Wonderful," she replied. "Now I want you to tell me your name, your favourite tree and why you are here.

I need the rest of the group to be respectful and keep any confidences that are disclosed today."

Eleanor began, "My name is Eleanor and I'm here to heal myself of bad experiences and relationships. My favourite tree is the Oak"

"Ahh, the Oak is King of the woods, associated with strength and endurance. What makes you happy,

Eleanor? she asked, and, hesitatingly Eleanor replied with a smile, "My dog, Barney".

"Excellent, thank you for sharing that with us. Now who is next?"

"I'm Jude and my favourite tree is the Hazel".

"Thank you, Hazel is the tree of wisdom and knowledge, and can you tell us what you would like to achieve by being here? What makes you happy, Jude?

"I want to feel more attuned to nature as I live in the city. I dream of a life in the country. Reading is my favourite thing to do, so I can live in the fantasy lands of my books and escape to rustic places", said Jude.

"Excellent", replied Yolanda.

Lastly, Anna spoke, "My tree is the Pine. I'm here because I've been ill but I'm in remission now; I believe that trees may have powers of healing." Without being prompted she went on to say," the feeling of sunshine on my face makes me happy".

Yolanda responded, "The Pine tree is a tree of heights, of aspirations and far-seeing. Thank you all, we are almost ready to set off. We will take 30 minutes to walk to our first stopping place where I will ask you to find a tree with which you feel some affinity. Please don't talk, but listen to the sounds of the woods in order to appreciate a holistic experience"

Yolanda led them onwards, replicating movements akin to t'ai chi; though no-one dared to laugh, they were all inwardly amused. The party advanced at snail's pace, listening to murmurings of the wind and bird calls. The woodland floor felt soft and springy underfoot, their steps buffered by mossy foliage and dried pine needles. The occasional noise of a snapping of twig was sharply heard. Jude stopped to look closely at a face in the bark of a tree and Anna observed a black and yellow striped caterpillar that was wriggling about its daily business.

Now they had reached Yolanda's spot of choice. "Gather around," she softly called. "This is where we truly relax, for trees can turn negative energy into positive energy. Let us rest for a few moments in preparation for the most meaningful act of the day, where you will all hug a tree! This will increase your levels of oxytocin, serotonin and dopamine to produce a natural high, a feeling of happiness and bonding. I want you to select your tree: take your time to find the right one to build a relationship with, whether it be a fat beech tree or a slim horse chestnut. Remember that we take some of the most important things for granted, for example, water, air and trees that are necessary for survival. Material objects cannot bring us true contentment and we must seek to find happiness within ourselves. This is your chance to truly reconnect with our earth. Now, please, go and select your tree!"

The ladies looked around for potentially pleasing trunk partners. After a few minutes they all stood under their chosen one. "Put your arms around your trees. Think of that vast network of communicating roots beneath you; those roots are talking to each other, sharing water and nutrients. Feel the energy vibration travelling up through your toes, legs, chest, and all the way up to your head. Put your face right up to the bark and breathe in the woody essential oils that are emitted.

Feel the roughness against your skin. Your tree has an energy vibration that emits an aura of safety and stability. Close your minds to everything else, breathe slowly and deeply, concentrate, tap into that vibe. We will now silently honour our trees!" Yolanda had almost induced her own trance-like state.

The hugging continued, each person was certainly having an unique experience whilst wondering about that of the others. Aided at last by rhythmic respiration they slowly began to absorb the positive synergy they yearned. Refreshed now, Yolanda calmly brough the session to a close. "Come and sit with me for our debrief. Is everyone alright? This can be very emotional for some". Then seeing that no-one was drying up tears, she gave them permission to breathe normally, so as to help them become grounded once again. "Now I'm not going to ask about your experiences as I believe these feelings should remain private to us all. I hope you won't mind helping me to conclude this session by standing up and shouting, Say it once and say it loud,

I'm a tree hugger and I'm proud!" and with that she jumped back in her campervan and disappeared through the clearing. Eleanor, Jude and Anna took one look at each other and exploded into laughter. It was a wonderful release as they had all stifled the feeling for the last two hours. Each time they tried to stop they were unable and they were riding high on its infectiousness, laughing until they could hardly breathe. Finally Jude cut in, "Well I've had an amazing time, I'm feeling on top of the world," and the others spontaneously began singing "Looking down on creation and the only explanation I can find...."

"Hey, what about, "I hugged a tree and I liked it....it felt so wrong, it felt so right!". With this clear evidence of bonding Eleanor suggested that they head off for a drink if they were all in agreement.

A little bit of ethereal healing had certainly taken place in all of them when they ventured into the woods, and in ways they could not have anticipated.

Wildlife

There is a mystical 'she shed' at the bottom of a garden, in a place that is larger than a village but smaller than a town. It is neither rural or urban, bordering on woodland with a river flowing through. It is not the sort of place where you might expect a witch to reside, but a witch cannot be defined by where she lives or how she expresses her spirituality. She is defined by her affinity with the natural world. Imagine a modern day Green Witch if you can; they exist in various forms in the unlikeliest of places. She identifies with the name Hecate (He-cah-tee), Goddess of the Witches, and she lives by the Rede of 'do as you will and harm none'.

Dedicated to the power of natural magic and healing through herbs and flowers she is completely at one with nature. She knows secrets of the earth, fire, water and air, and how to create spells, potions and healing teas. Her days on the planet follow a nature themed calendar of solar and seasonal festivals, committing to their associated customs and rituals. In the evenings the shed is illuminated with solar lights; she adorns the surrounding decked area with candle lit lanterns, creating a temple-like feel. A beaded curtain swished to one side reveals a cosy seated area and hanging on the walls are pictures of woodland scenes and their wildlife inhabitants. She has drawn these pictures of her animal friends in stunning detail for she knows intimately every feather, bright eye, whisker and wet nose they possess. Around the time of sunset through to darkness they come to her, not just for the food she provides, as they are capable of foraging for themselves. It is for reasons far greater; they are animal guides, magical aids who love their Beautiful Earth Mamma. She awaits their nightly arrival with anticipation, Mr Truffles the Badger, Merle the Raven and Flareon the Fox. She would never, ever admit it but the fox is her favourite, the one to whom she is most spiritually connected. Closing her eyes in concentration, she senses that he is coming to her. Flareon is indeed first to call, he has left his woodland wild, slinking through the foliage and checking to see who is there. He is happy now because he knows he will be lifted into Beautiful Earth Mamma's arms to be fussed and nuzzled. His loveliness makes her heart sing, his peppery brush tail is magnificent, his eyes are soulful and intelligent. They metamorphose into one another as he becomes entangled in her long red hair, sharing a sense of togetherness and peace. Soon they will hear the whispering of raven wings and the croaking call that announces the arrival of Merle. He flies onto her shoulder and makes himself comfortable there, delivering beaky kisses to her cheek. His feathers have a marvellous ebony sheen and his insightful, beady eyes perceive every detail. He is her trusted messenger who connects the material world with the spirit world's magical forces. Mr Truffles the badger leaves his set when he feels good and ready. Governed by the time the sun sets he comes out to forage and socialise. He has plenty of time this summer evening before the moon is bright. Beautiful Earth Mamma likes best his wiry whiskers and large black nose. His stocky body is covered in grey-white hair and his tail is very short. His dark eyes punctuate his black striped head. When she looks into them she feels a depth of trust and understanding which is pleasing beyond measure. When all were present, supper was served on the deck. The animals nibbled and nudged around, as polite as friends at a dining table. They were treated to a woodland smorgasbord of cereals, fruit, nuts and bulbs then remained together watching the new moon and looking out for shooting stars.

At the local hospital on Ward 1b a hullabaloo has broken out. Dedicated Sister Martha Stevens is in the ugly midst of it. She lovingly looks after her patients on the Care of the Elderly ward and does not take kindly to anyone or anything that comes in the way of this. Wednesday afternoons have recently been looked forward to as 'cream tea day', possibly more so by the staff, as the patients rarely have insight into which day of the week it is. The ladies from the Royal Voluntary Service agreed to provide the ingredients and to serve the treat to the patients. All was going well until the Matron for Infection Control blasted through the ward doors like the coldest wind from Antarctica, and then trouble ensued.

The serving ladies stood frozen in time, waiting for the confrontation. When it came it was quite brutal. "What's happening here?" she bellowed. Matron McNally (otherwise known as Matron McNasty) was most definitely on the warpath.

The WRVS lady who was of a particularly nervous disposition dropped the plates, leaving a creamy, jammy splatter all over the corridor. She got such a fright that she felt a little bit of urine coursing down her leg. The smashed crockery splintered in all directions. The elderly patients stood as still as statues when the music stops.

"Who has dared to bring these scones in here? The patients will get Campylobacter food poisoning from the cream and if they've been made in a dirty kitchen with poor hygiene we'll have a diarrhoea outbreak to manage, all your fault but my responsibility to deal with, as I'm in charge of all of this!" Her arms gesticulated wildly as her face blushed puce. Matron McNasty was furious! The WRVS lady started crying and rushed off to the toilet, closely followed by the others.

"Come on luvvies, let's get you back to your beds and I'll put the Perry Como CD on for you. We'll have a nice cup of tea and a sing-a-long when we've settled down," said Sister Marsha. The ward domestic whistled the tune of Magic Moments and casually cleared up the mess. In the ward office Sister Marsha maintained her professionalism by stifling her anger at Matron McNally. She couldn't help but slam the door shut. What should have been a positive experience for her patients had yet again turned into an embarrassing charade. The time had come to speak out, to retaliate.

"I would appreciate it if you would be respectful on my ward and discuss your issues away from our patients. You have needlessly upset us all today", Marsha said, then continuing, "Last month you caused me dreadful embarrassment when the Pets As Therapy dogs were visiting. It had all been properly agreed, a policy was written and approved so we could even have monkeys and goats on the premises if need be, and you ordered them off the ward. You called those dogs scruffy little beasts. They are NOT scruffy little beasts, they were washed and groomed prior to the visit. They are very well behaved, they cheer my patients up and have a calming effect on them. I'm sick of your interference and I'm reporting you to the Head of Nursing, now get off my ward!!"

"I'm only doing my job!", exclaimed Matron McNally, "and you will find I have the full support of the senior management team!" That was the end of their noxious exchange. There had been a string of misdemeanours over the last few weeks which Sister Marsha had not been brave enough to address. Now she was crying tears of frustration and shaking with temper. This could not continue any longer, it was time to take action. Sister Marsha is the god-daughter of Hecate. Having no one else to turn to in relation to her defunct relationship with Matron McNally, she discusses it with Hecate over a dandelion and camomile tea. "I need your help, the managers won't support me *because she is one of them.* She is a bully who people won't stand up to. I don't know how or why she ever became a nurse. She gets away with being horrible all the time and I'm so fed up because of her. She won't make me leave my job, though".

Wise Hecate understands that such people exist only to make the lives of others a misery. She also knows exactly who Matron McNally is, as she is her 'next door but one' neighbour. Hecate heard her shooing away the wildlife from her garden and recently had thrown stones at Mr Truffle who reported her heinous act. Something had to be done. The planning process swung into action.

Hecate pulls on her green velvet gown which is only worn at special times in the calendar, the Solstices and Equinoxes. It is a full-length hooded garment embroidered with bees, ferns and wildlife friends. Leaving her hair free she puts on the headdress made only from nature's wares. She collected rowan, hawthorn, birch and roses and lovingly fashioned the crown. On wearing it she feels harmony and magic flowing through her from top to toe. She reminds herself that *whatever energy a person puts into the world, be it positive or negative, will be returned to that person three times over.* She feels spiritually authorised to call upon her healing powers.

Next she prepares an altar, placing a white cloth on a wide shelf. A torch is lit at either side, a candle positioned in the middle. Ornamental likenesses of Merle, Flareon and Mr Truffles are set in front of the candle. She has made a spell jar containing lavender oil, garlic cloves, Himalayan salt, amber and turmeric. On a mini scroll is written a secret spell which cannot be shared. Sage incense burns, its function is to clear any negative energy. In the woods Mr Truffle's nose twitches, Flareon's tail switches, Merle ruffles his feathers: their presence has been requested and it's time to go.

On the decked area Hecate briefs them, for some work needs to be done as a team, summoning all of their powers of creativity and intuition. They are going on a special mission to Matron McNasty's garden where they have special tasks to perform. Merle is going to fly over to make sure she isn't presently sitting there. Most summer nights when the weather is warm she has been having a glass or two of wine outside. This will be of importance later, but for now they need to know if the coast is clear. Once given the squawk, Flareon will walk along her fence, jump into her garden and leave a charm bag concealed beneath a bush. This does not contain anything harmful. It is filled with acorns, herbs and crystals which are magically charged. Hecate places the drawstring of the bag between his teeth, knowing that he can comfortably transport it there.

A special preparation of cinnamon, cayenne pepper and rosemary has to be sprinkled around the doors and windows to help draw out negative energies. Mr Truffles is going to squeeze under the fence and be helped by Merle to scatter the contents of a little muslin bag. The rest of the work will be carried out solely by Merle over the next few evenings. This will involve the carriage of small vials of calming and endorphin producing powder which will infuse, unnoticed into Matron McNasty's wine. There will be nightly spell incantations and candle ceremonies to encourage the flow of positive energies.

The hospital staff began to notice a very slight change in Matron McNally's demeanour. She has been giving the odd smile here and there and is not scowling and barking at people as she did. She offered to lend a useful book to one of her colleagues and swapped a shift just to be helpful. On her way home from work she stopped to give a colleague a lift. This generated great interest among the nurses who noted these subtle changes. Matron McNally began to feel good, she was sleeping very well and was newly energised. With each positive act came an enhanced feeling of contentment she had never experienced before.

Marsha tells Hecate that her life is so much better now. She explains that Matron McNally has become quite pleasant. She has even apologised for all that happened in the past, acknowledging she had not been a nice person. Matron McNally was accepting a new job at a neighbouring hospital and looking forward to a fresh start. "All I wanted was for her to be civil," Marsha stated. " I didn't need her to leave. Did you cast the wrong spell or one that was too powerful? she asked.

Hecate laughed, "No my dear, the spell worked perfectly and was exactly as intended. I didn't drive her away, I unblocked her energy channels. When she discovered her inner happiness she was able to take charge of her destiny. I always use my gift carefully to channel my energies into positive healing. Sometimes you may not feel the love that surrounds you or that miracles can happen. Cherish those you love, both people and animals. Open your mind to things that are not tangible or orthodox and you may find that magical synchronicity flows through you.

Green Love

I shall call you Allium Ampeloprasum, if I may, even though it sounds a little grand. You will look dazzling when I have finished all of our preparations. I will take you to the village hall, the gardening club and the country club but only when the time is right for us. I will bed you in firm, moist earth because I know you will flourish there. Creeping at sunrise I see your beautiful white bulb and rich green tip glistening with frost and dream of holding you, singing the labours of our summer evenings. Sometimes I feel insecure, worrying that another may steal you away, or that you will be ravaged by smut or downy mildew, but long after we have wilted and gone to seed I will love you, my hardy biennial.

Huldufolk Hidden People

Kirstin Olafsdottir has agreed to give an interview on a subject that is close to her heart, and that of thousands of other Icelanders. She has invited BBC Earth journalist Trude Leif into her basic though homely cottage that sits in the lowlands of a glacial river, shadowed by majestic mountains. Her home is somewhat sheltered in the valley, though still at the mercy of the elements inherent in this dramatic landscape. Such a hostile environment of twisted volcanic rocks, hot spring geysers and rough terrain surely commands respect from the local inhabitants. Their lives and imaginations are dominated by weather conditions born of powerful natural phenomena.

On entering the warm lounge, Trude began to peel off several layers of clothes that had protected her from the bitterly cold winds, her chestnut hair tumbled free. Glancing around the room she noticed a lit candle on the window sill and a lava lamp burning on the sideboard behind her. The walls were adorned with pictures of indigenous flowers and wildlife and a row of colourful cushions rested on the sofa. They sat at the table together and Kirstin offered Trude a brew of some special healing tea that was gifted to her by elf friend Pulta.

Kirstin has typical Nordic looks, mid length blonde hair and blue eyes that are framed by stylish spectacles. She is quietly spoken and her command of English is excellent. "You want to know more about the folklore of the Huldufolk and the elves?" she asks Trude. Her eyes are lit up, smiling genuinely at the prospect of sharing her experiences and her speech is steady in its recall of events.

"When I was a little girl playing in the fields I wanted to climb up high on a certain boulder, even though my friends told me not to. My foot slipped on some slippery wet moss and as I fell, I bit my lip. It poured with blood and we felt this was a penance for disturbing an elf dwelling. I heard a voice calling from the rock and as I drew nearer I saw a little person which I recognised to be an elf," she said.

Trude is astonished and stops to ask, "And how did you know that?" She had just remembered to take out her notebook and began fumbling in her backpack. Kirstin continues, "My Grandmother Amma told me stories of the elves and the Huldufolk that are embedded in our Icelandic culture; they are supernatural beings who live in enchanted rocks and cliffs within a parallel world. They keep livestock, row fishing boats and pick wild crowberries. Amma was able to communicate with them in both psychic and telepathic ways. She told me that humans see little and believe even less, and that children who are more attuned to seeing hidden people would later lose this ability. Others who are lucky enough to retain this psychic gift will remain in connection, sometimes maintaining lifelong relationships. The elves and Hidden People are naturally capricious and can make themselves visible at will. They will only show themselves to certain folk, sometimes when angered, or to warn of impending danger. Sometimes they would warn children to return home if they had wandered too far away, so they try to protect us. They seek to live a harmonious existence unless disturbed or upset, so you must never throw rocks which could cause them harm. Due to their mysterious powers they are to be revered and respected." Trude's eyes are wide in wonder. She wants to laugh but must remain serene and professional. She asks, "Is there a difference between elves and Huldufolk?"

Kirstin explains, "Very much so! Elves are small in stature with large ears, their size varies between five centimetres to almost three metres in height. Huldufolk are more likened to humans, they are taller and slimmer than us, also finer looking, more alluring and of freer spirit. They dress in green and grey clothing such as was worn here in the 19th century." She takes a small book from the shelf and shows it to Trude. Pointing to a picture she says, "This story is about my elf friend, Ryvvik, but that is not how he really looks. He did not want a true picture of himself on these pages. He doesn't want to frighten anyone and prefers to be anonymous," she explains, laughing for the first time.

"How do we know what they look like, if they are hidden?" asks Trude.

"Well from witness accounts we have put together all of the descriptions from elf encounters. From this correlated information we have identified at least seventy different types of elves! Facts mixed with folklore, recollections of elf sightings have been passed down through generations. I attained a degree at theElfskoll at Reykjavik University. This level of educational achievement plus my personal encounters makes me quite an authority on the subject. I am an official elf whisperer! Afterall, such is my commitment to the elves, I was prepared to go to prison for them, but we will come back to that as there are other things I'd like to tell you.

Trude asked, "Are there any particular times of the year that are associated with sightings?"

Kirsten explains," Well there are four days in the year that have a special connection to the elves. Firstly there is Christmas Night, then New Year's Eve. On 6th January, which is the last day of Christmas, our children dress up as elves and they take flaming torches, walking in a procession to one of the many local elf bonfires, alfabrenna. The Elf King and Queen ride through the countryside, visiting the bonfires, to see people do elf dances and sing elf songs. Afterwards there are fireworks to mark the end of the Christmas celebrations. According to legend, elves make themselves visible to humans on this day, strange things happen on that night, such as talking cows and seals who take on a human form! Around midnight the cows all stand up and speak to each other in nonsensical rhyming couplets; anyone who overhears them can be driven insane.

On Midsummer Night, folklore warns that if you sit at crossroads, elves will attempt to seduce you with food and jewels. There will be grave consequences for accepting their offers but great rewards for resisting." Kirstin pauses and takes a few sips of tea.

Trude also takes the opportunity to drink some tea for she has been scribbling away in her notebook. She is wondering how she is going to write up all of this fanciful detail. "Kirstin, can you tell me of the problem about the road building and the trouble it caused you? She asked.

"Well that was a very interesting but stressful time", Kirstin further explained, "There are many oddly shaped rocks in an ancient lava field which is about a ten minute drive outside of Reykjavik. Many of us Friends of the Lava environmentalists feel a special affinity with the stunning waterfalls, wildlife and plants here. We felt we had to protest against a new highway development that would run right through the Alfholl (Elf Hill) settlement. Supernatural forces exist here and a very important elf church was to be destroyed by the road builders. This elf church lies in an enchanted spot and is connected by light energy to other churches and other places. The elves are very territorial and protective of their dwelling places and if left alone are perfectly harmless. On the other hand, damage or destruction of their properties upsets them and their wrath will manifest. Bad luck stories of curses abound, accidents, mechanical breakdown and even sudden death have all been brought about by angered elves. A construction worker broke his foot and a mechanical digger was overturned on a different road project that enraged the elves. So, we set up a camp at the site and discussed our concerns with the Icelandic Road and Coastal Administration, who were leading the project. We tried to explain that whilst the proposed highway would provide a more direct route to the peninsular, this would not be without cultural and environmental costs. We explained there could be dark disturbances that result from displacing supernatural forces and misfortune to those who destroy elf territory." Trude gasped, "Oh my, you are scaring me! So what happened next with the highway plan?"

Kirstin continued," I used telepathy to communicate with the elves and found there were three generations living inside those boulders and tussocks. My psychic friend and I asked if they would agree to being moved to an alternative location, and we had to wait until they were ready to negotiate with us. More and more environmentalists joined the blockade to prevent the start of the road work, keeping the bulldozers back until the elves began to collaborate. The police were called as we obstructed the site and some elf advocates, including myself were arrested! We were thrown into prison overnight and let out the next morning. I found it very distressing as I am amicable and a civil person, but it created publicity and the case was heard in the Supreme Court. The elves agreed to move out for a week in order for their boulder to be relocated a few meters away. This would allow the works to proceed. They specified that their boulder must be located in a grassy area, and that a view of the sea must be retained".

"And did the story end well?" asked Trude.

"Well, once the relocation was completed everything became peaceable one more", said Kirstin, laughing gently. "I have no doubt that future projects will provoke the elves and we will be fighting for them again. I believe it is vitally important that we respect them and try to live in harmony, they are so much a part of us, of our people."

Kirstin looked out of the window; suddenly clapping her hands she exclaimed," The sky has come alive for you tonight, Trude. Have you ever experienced the Aurora Borealis, The Northern Lights? Come and see!" and she took Trude by the hand and led her into the garden.

Trude looked up in wonderment at the most stunning natural light display. She could see the green striations changing into white, pink and purple particle streams, the sky so dramatically illuminated. She felt so lucky and honoured that the conditions were perfectly synchronised to produce this amazing phenomena. Last year her friends had booked an expensive trip to Iceland

but did not get to experience this. With tears running down her face she turned to Kirsten and said, "I feel so honoured!"
Kirstin was laughing and so happy to share the moment with Trude.
"At times like this I feel such an emotional connection with nature and the elements, it is part of my identity. I want to protect the environment and continue to educate about the hidden people, as they are also an integral part of me", explained Kirsten. The lights began to fade and the sky returned to its dark and starry state.
"Thank you so much for allowing me to interview you," Trude said. "When I leave Iceland I will always keep this special memory with me, as well as having a more open mind for things that cannot be explained. I feel it's possible that such beings can exist, that aren't always tangible, there are some things we cannot always perceive. The hidden people have not made themselves visible to me, but that does not mean they are not real. I will carry these thoughts with me and follow the future

stories of the elves and Huldufolk, for as you said, I believe they will have more to tell us".

Shapeshifter

Sean anticipated the advent of the Seventh Stream, just as the arrival of the strawberry moon and dark purple sea purported to it. The sun had almost peaked at its most northerly position in the sky and he had so far counted seven days in a row of high tides. The time of the earliest sunrise had already occurred. He believed in new beginnings and that the evolutionary changes of nature are gifted by the solstice, a celebration of life and love. The longest day of the year was approaching. For those who tilled the land it highlighted the halfway point between planting and harvest, and for seafarers it indicated the coming of lobster season.

The days between June and September were the best times to catch the strong yet sweet-flavoured blue shellfish. He baited the pots with salted herring and set them on the foreshore among the gullies and rocky prominences. The low tide times were especially important, for that was when he retrieved the pots and claimed his bounty. Sometimes the catch consisted only of the smallest, entrapped crustaceans. Sean was grateful for whatever he caught, whether it be crawfish or crabs; either one provided food on the table and a small income. He never tired of feasting on the pinkish flesh served with chunks of bread, or with boiled potatoes and green beans pulled fresh from his growing patch. On fine weather days he sailed his boat out between the piers. The dory was made in traditional style with a lightweight bottom and high sides. Hand painted on the side was the name *'Maid Meredith'* and this was the only visible evidence that connected Sean to a human form who once existed; the name of the only woman that he had ever loved, and so devastatingly lost. He felt safe in the boat as it cut cleanly through the waves, throwing into the air a spittle of salty foam. A bob of inquisitive seals began to follow and frolic alongside the boat. Sean always felt privileged when this happened and he sat back, quietly observing them. He knew it was unwise to stare into those huge eyes, for the seal should control the encounter and not be intimidated, though he did so anyway. One of the seals reared up from the water, clapping and slapping its flippers and tail. The dark eyes seemed to peer into his very soul, the wiry whiskers twitching in mock conversation. He was mesmerised by its expression and percussive sounds as its sleek, dappled form surfed the waves. He watched until the pod grew tired of tailgating, choosing instead to haul out and bask on the rocks. A strange feeling descended upon him which he could not shake off. The advent was so very near; his greatest wish was to see Meredith one more time, though he felt unworthy of that chance. He reflected that a liar and a cheat does not deserve reward, and that sadly, what was done cannot be undone.

Sean returned to his lofty, cliff top cottage overlooking the sandy bay. On wild weather days the wind howled around it though was unable to penetrate its robust stonework. In the smugglers' coves beneath, the air hung damp and silently still. The roaring, whispering conversation of the ocean was his ever-present companion; its evolving rhythms and hues animated purely by natural forces. In the evening Sean lit an oil lamp and kept watch across the bay. The bluish night lights dimly glowed through the windows of the Marine Laboratory. Few people knew the purpose of the research building that nestled at the foot of the cliff, or what was stored and studied there in the ambient temperature aquarium tanks. Sometimes Sean took a tot of brandy in the evening for relaxation purposes, though not lately. He had to remain alert to carry out his intensive surveillance of the beachy cove. The moon was at its highest and brightest, its luminescence that evening was unique. Something caught his attention on the shoreline and his heart began racing. He saw a figure emerge seamlessly from the sea. Its lithe, silky body transitioned through the stages of therianthropy, casting off a grey skin cloak. Once free of its epidermis, a human form emerged from the foamy waves. The Selkie maiden stepped cautiously onto land, moving gingerly at first and re-connecting with the texture of sand beneath her feet. She quickly gained confidence, and like a springing antelope leapt through the air with joyful inhibition.

Sean ran from the cottage, blundering and stumbling down the rugged cliff path as if his life depended upon it. He had waited so long to see her, not even knowing if Meredith would ever return.

"Meredith, Meredith," he called and her name resounded around the still bay. The figure immediately snatched up her sealskin, grasping it protectively against her body. She would never be deceived again, as she had been once before.

Seven years ago she left her submarine sanctuary within the occult reefs and coves to exercise her powers to walk on land. The exuberance she experienced on exiting the sea was indescribable. How could she have been so reckless to lay out her seal skin on a rock and so frivolous to sing and dance? She was self-absorbed in the liberating experience and caught up in the moment.

Meredith's voice carried on the breeze, its sweet notes were both captivating and seductive. Sean's senses were infiltrated by the exclusive sound and in that moment he knew he must find a way to make her stay with him. At the onset of their first encounter Meredith made it perfectly clear that she could not and would not remain indefinitely. She explained that her visit would be time limited and that ultimately she must return to the sea. Meredith had been honest with him; as a water deity she could exist only briefly on land, requiring the sea to recharge her energies. Sean was captivated by her beauty and closed his mind to the fact that anything untoward could happen, let alone that she would leave him heartbroken. He seized the moment, swiftly grabbing her discarded seal skin, and in doing so, trapped her and made her enslaved to him; without it she was unable to return to the ocean.

The days turned to weeks and Meredith's time on dry land was fast running out. As her constitution weakened and her powers drained she had begged Sean to return her pelt from the laboratory. "What is the point of holding me prisoner here?" she pleaded. "I will die soon if you don't help to return me to the sea. Haven't you heard of the saying, *"if you love someone, let them go, for if they return, they were always yours and if they don't, they never were?"*

But Sean could not, would not let her go. When Meredith realised that he had made her situation untenable she began making plans to escape. In a distraught state Meredith swam as far as she could through the dark waters, her transonic distress calls rang out over the ocean. She knew that the senses of the Selkie seal maidens were perfectly attuned to her siren acoustics. First to respond was Ceasg, maid of the waves, whose special powers allowed her to grant wishes and good fortune. Meredith must make her understand that she had been robbed of her pelt and that it was imperative for her to return to the sea. Meredith knew she was doomed unless she could find a way to turn this grave situation around. Sometimes it may be possible to retrieve the skin of a recently deceased seal and to rejuvenate it. This was her greatest chance of survival. Meredith knew that her own pelt was stored in a secure cabinet at The Marine Laboratory and she was unable to reclaim what was rightfully hers. She knew that Sean had deliberately taken it there where she would never be allowed to gain access to it. The research scientist's hands had greedily grabbed it from Sean, so desperate was he to take charge of something so exquisite. It would be stored securely in a locked tank while the team researched its esoteric properties.

Meredith asked Ceasg if she could bring to her a seal pelt in any condition from any source, as time was of the essence. She had never asked for such a favour before though had helped others with similar requests. Ceasg understood the urgency of her plea and promised to enlist the help of their fellow Selkies in the retrieval of a seal skin. Once found, the pelt would undergo a unique process of metamorphosis to restore its shape shifting properties. She knew what she must do; she placed the seal skin on a driftwood altar when the sun reached nautical twilight at six degrees below the horizon. Crepuscular animals are most active during this period and supernatural powers are at their most potent. Each cell in sequence passed on its energy to the next, until the whole skin was re-perfused and revitalised. Ceasg wrapped it around Meredith and adjusted it to her form and then watched as Meredith was liberated by the sea and swam effortlessly once more. Meredith had also been waiting for the optimum tide conditions. Should she come back, should she not? It was a difficult decision but another seven years would have to elapse before another chance would present itself. Time had not altered her beauty, or perhaps she was rejuvenated through the process of metamorphosis. Her phthalo-green eyes were as mesmerising as ever, her hair the colour of viridis-black which twined about her torso like a cloak of cloying kelp. She had the capability to influence and change the elements of nature. She was, at best, a mischievous siren with the ability to hypnotise and seduce. Her darker powers were such that she was able to conjure up a storm and drown sailors and fishermen in their own nets should she choose to do so. Shaun underestimated her, never believing she would exercise these abilities but he was gullible; a fool who believed that Meredith had returned to him out of love and forgiveness. He was weak and incautious after years of longing for her, now made giddy by her presence.

"Sean, I have found a way for us to be together forever! I can make your soul immortal," she tantalised. He felt helpless under her spell.

"Come with me and I will show you the watery caverns and caves that I inhabit. I will show you my world and bestow on you the most exclusive ability to shapeshift." Her incantation infiltrated him and insidiously possessed him. Meredith reached out to Shaun. The touch of her hand was surprisingly warm against his cheek. Sean declared, "My life has been empty without you. In my dreams you returned to me and only then did I feel whole again. I doubted you would grant me another chance after my terrible indiscretion. It was terribly wrong of me to steal your pelt and I can see that so clearly now. That act was not born out of love but pure selfishness and I was a fool. Take me with you to the places you described so that I can see them for myself. Allow me to experience your world and let me stay with you," he pleaded, taking her hand and remembering its shape and fit within his. She drew him into the lapping waves and he followed willingly. Her lips touched his and her breath became his. "Come now, you have transitioned! I have granted you the gift of underwater respiration, through gills, but you must maintain your concentration. In just a single moment of inattention you could lose the ability to breathe," she warned. Sean's lungs emptied and there was a snorting expulsion of breath from his nostrils before he submerged himself. The new breathing technique flooded his cells, making them oxygen rich; the physiological change produced psychedelic waves of euphoria. They swam together through the green rippling ribbons and coralline algae. Sean marvelled at the violet iridescence of the Irish moss. He gazed in wonder at the silvery flashes of fish that darted all around him and gasped at the luminescence of a giant octopus that brushed close by. A wave of fear ran through him at the prospect of encountering gnashing shark teeth or stinging jellyfish in this unknown marine territory. Meredith swam effortlessly in her natural habitat with Sean following in the slipstream. Suddenly she indicated to him that they needed to surface. A mist had descended over the ocean, bringing with it a sense of stillness and foreboding. In the distance a weather-beaten galleon ship with tattered sails cut silently through the water. An eerie orange glow emitted from a swinging lantern high above the poop deck of the ghost ship. “It's time,” said Meredith. “Time for what?” asked Sean with a feeling of growing unease. “Time for you to meet the crew and join ship”, she explained.

“A cruise?” he enquired, “I wasn't expecting this...”

“Indeed, a cruise... of sorts,” replied Meredith, “I've brought you to the ship of the doomed, a ship of lost souls. All those aboard live in a state of perpetual punishment for wronging others through their selfish deceptions. Every person here is trapped in limbo, in this watery holding zone between heaven and hell. You stole my skin and now I've stolen your soul. You shall never return to dry land, just as you prevented my return to the sea. Now is the time of reckoning and you must understand that I did not return to you out of love or forgiveness, as you thought of, and dreamed of. I came back in the name of retribution. I'm going to leave you now. You will remain here while you repent and one day, *when and if I see fit*, I may release your soul. Now, climb aboard and accept your fate on ‘*The Navem Mortuorum*’, the Ship of the Dead”.

Still As a Statue

Stonemasonry runs through the veins of Desmond Pennington, he is a master of this ancient craft. Carving shapes from stone is how he makes a living, but it is also his passion. He has used his artistic ability to chisel life forms into marble and granite, creating statues of humans, animals, specially commissioned designs for the rich and famous.

As a child, Desmond's father used to read him Greek Mythology stories. His favourite was that of Pygmalion's Statue which had inspired him to produce the highest quality, life-like forms he could fashion. Pygmalion was alleged to be not only a king of Cyprus but a fine sculptor who looked in vain for his perfect woman. All around him were disastrous marriages which led him to the decision that he would never marry, but would devote all his love and inspiration into creating statues of beauty. He made a marble statue of a girl so perfect that he fell in love with her, adorning her with flower garlands and jewellery, praying to the goddess

Aphrodite that she would grant his statue the gift of life. In his workshop she remained lifeless and cold, eyes staring past him. In despair he kissed her lips then fell asleep at her feet. In his dream he kissed her again, but this time he felt warmth flowing through her. She moved gently, returning his love and enfolding soft arms around him. On waking he found the beautiful girl in place of his statue. Aphrodite appeared to him, explaining that she had granted his wish for a happiness he had himself fashioned, his own queen.

In contrast to the Greek myth, Desmond had been lucky in love. He had received a high profile order from a wealthy customer, Lord Bramton, owner of a Northumberland country estate and after many months the piece of work was now complete. When delivering The sculpture, he met Shirley, Lord Bramton's housekeeper. Their meeting was unusual as it took place in the middle of the night. The commissioned piece was of Peter Pan, the favourite fairytale character of his young daughter Emmeline whose adventures had captured her imagination. Lord Bramton wanted the statue to be installed at this time so it would appear 'magically', in the morning, just as when the original Peter Pan of Kensington Gardens was inaugurated. Soon Peter would become an exquisite feature of the walled garden, a mystical symbol of eternal youth. Lord Bramton had also requested that a series of wildlife and fairy sculptures be added periodically, for the ongoing amusement and entertainment of his beloved daughter. Shirley was very admiring of the Peter Pan statue and made sure she provided many cups of tea for Desmond whilst he carried out the statue's installation. As the further orders were placed by Lord Bramton, he ventured back and forth to the estate and began to look forward to seeing Shirley's smiling eyes, chestnut hair and engaging smile. They started going out together and Lord Bramton found himself advertising for a new housekeeper some months later when Shirley announced that she was going to marry Desmond. Two years later they were delighted to welcome their son

William into the world, and as he preferred to be called Billy, the shortened version of his name stuck. Billy grew into a sensitive, introverted child who didn't make friends easily. He loved reading and researching things that were of interest to him and could easily become lost in a world of his own. He demonstrated some artistic traits in the form of line drawings and sketches and enjoyed hanging around his Dad's workshop, monitoring the works in progress. Desmond introduced him to the tools of his trade but Billy had not inherited the fine motor skills that are required to produce exacting work and they both became frustrated by his lack of aptitude. An alternative career in architecture was considered but Billy couldn't achieve the necessary grades to set him on this path. He channelled his interests into learning about famous sculptures such as Michelangelo's David and Our Lady of Lourdes, making a list of places to visit, to get close to the statues and maybe touch them. Billy found it difficult to initially secure jobs and then to remain employed, having been 'let go' on a couple of occasions due to poor time keeping and unauthorised days of absence. He was a dreamer who sang to his own tune. Lacking in ambition he drifted along, accepting cash loans from his Dad which they both knew would never be repaid. Desmond and Shirley worried about his lack of drive and focus and wondered if he would ever establish himself. It greatly disappointed Desmond that the family business would not be handed on; after many generations he began to accept it would be the end of the road for Pennington and Son. With a growing obsession and little finance to support any trips, Billy became increasingly restless and insular. Desmond became frustrated with him hanging around aimlessly, day after day. Then one evening a certain news item sparked Billy's imagination and filled him with curiosity. Across Ireland in various locations there were reports of a phenomenon, of moving statues of the Virgin Mary. A local woman was walking past the shrine with her daughters. They stopped to pray and were astonished to see that the idol, The Lady of Lourdes appeared to be breathing or singing and her hands were moving! As news spread of the event thousands of people made the journey there, hoping to see the spectacle for themselves, believing it to be a miracle. Billy obsessed over how this could happen, was it an illusion, a trick of the light, or was it really a religious message communicated by the Blessed Virgin Mary herself?

Many people in the crowd claimed to have witnessed the vision. Billy wondered if it was a case of mass hysteria, when a group of people experience similar manifestations, whether real or imaginary. Many people swore they saw something, a smile or a slight movement of her head. They gave witness reports to the television interviewers which whipped up even greater interest. The stories became even more outlandish with one gentleman claiming he saw the face of the Pope transposed over that of the Virgin Mary. So intriguing and baffling were the reports that Billy decided to personally investigate them. He would ask his Dad for a cash advance so he could make the journey to Ireland.

Billy visited the places that had received the most publicity of the sightings. Everywhere he went there were crowds of people clutching rosary beads, gazing trance-like, at the religious icons, looking for a sign. He elbowed his way to the front of the crowd, determined to get a close-up view and hardly daring to blink in case he missed any slight movement. The atmosphere was intense, the believers appeared to outnumber the non-believers. Billy wondered if these people were really sharing a religious experience, could it be that their belief was so strong that they imagined it or were they hallucinating? All around him were prayers muttered in low tones, group recitations of the Rosary began to mesmerise him and infiltrate his thoughts. Suddenly he experienced a feeling of electricity running right through his body then he noticed a string of firefly-type lights swooping down, forming an illuminated crown above the Virgin Mary's head. The Virgin Mary tilted her head skywards. Gasps and cries of astonishment at the amazing sight rippled through the crowd and then, overwhelmed by the experience, Billy's legs crumpled and he fell to the ground. He came around to a sea of faces peering into his own. Two strong men pulled him to his feet and sat him down on a tree stump at the foot of the grotto. A hip flask filled with whiskey was pressed to his lips. He felt groggy at first but then feelings of warmth, love and enlightenment coursed through him. He felt euphoric, shouting out that he'd seen it, the crown of lights, and he'd felt the presence of a higher being.

The following day Billy felt different, as if with renewed energy and a positive outlook he had never experienced before. He decided to have a snack in the city park before making his return journey home. Wandering along the path he noticed how green the trees were and how the sun's shafts of light led him through the foliage. The path widened out to a picnic area at the foot of a large marble monument. Billy dropped his bag and climbed onto the base of the structure, then once close enough he touched the cool marble. The depicted subject had strong broad shoulders, he wore a tunic which fell in folded layers as he rested back on an anvil. The tools of his trade, hammer, tongs and chisel were grasped in powerful hands and he was looking up to the heavens. Billy felt an overwhelming connection with this sculpture, running his fingers over the smooth surfaces, taking in every detail as if he were learning Braille. He imagined the hammer beating down on the anvil in a fiery forge, its skilled movements creating alternative sculptures, the finest work that a stonemason could produce. He suddenly felt a force enter his body, an inexplicable transference of energy matter rippled through him. He felt that he was in telepathic communication with Hephaestus, Greek God of fire, stone masonry, patron of craftsmen. He was a kind and peace-loving God with the ability to make his creations move, a skill that he passed on to mortal artists.

Billy was filled with emotion and his tears dripped onto the stone, running in rivulets.

Billy climbed down and settled himself in the shade. He thought about his recent surreal experiences, trying to rationalise and understand them. Whatever had happened had definitely changed him, and for the better. He couldn't wait to return home to the workshop, to handle the tools with the skill and dexterity required to create objects of beauty. He knew he could do it now, and the gift he had been granted now filled him with enthusiasm and purpose.

The next morning, when Desmond arrived at the workshop he was incredulous to see Billy already chiselling away, making great progress with a new sculpture of his own design. He wanted to talk to Billy to find out how and why he had a change of heart about sculpting, and how Billy was now exhibiting such fine skill. Reluctant to interrupt, he merely watched from a distance, truly amazed at this creative change in Billy. Over the weeks that followed father and son worked alongside each other and their relationship both deepened and flourished. Desmond wanted to ask Billy about what happened in Ireland, as this was surely pivotal to the change that had occurred. Billy did not want to discuss his personal experiences and was actually questioning their validity, but knew that a transformation had surely happened. He poured everything into his work, applying every ounce of resourcefulness, imagination and ingenuity he possessed. Desmond already knew in his heart what Billy was shaping and fashioning, for it perfectly reflected a piece that he had previously made. When Billy completed his work of art, Desmond knew he had been right, and that the Wendy Darling statue would compliment that of his own statue, Peter Pan. Lord Bramton contacted Desmond, after years of sporadic communication. He explained that he had just become a Grandfather and that he would like Desmond to create an additional statue for the walled garden. This would be in celebration of the birth of his first grandchild, a baby girl named Syrinx, so named after a Greek forest nymph. A statue of Wendy to accompany Peter would be perfect. Desmond excitedly informed Lord Bramton that Billy had joined him in the family business and that they would like to offer him the chance to purchase a newly created Wendy statue. Then came such a revelation, that Peter Pan had brought the Bramton family years of pleasure, and in ways they could only have dreamed of. The best kept secret of the estate was never mentioned outside of family circles for it was so very special to them, bringing countless mysteries and joy. The last thing they wanted was for streams of visitors to crowd around on their private land. During certain summer nights, at twilight, hundreds of fireflies would congregate around Peter's head. This would always be a sign of a bewitching and truly amazing event about to unfold. At these times the family waited with bated breath, in anticipation of their mystical Peter coming to life and playing his Pan-pipes once more.

Mount Pleasant View

Mount Pleasant View is a residential nursing home, a care facility for those who are living out their twilight years. It is not built on a mount and it doesn't have much of a view, but aside from that, it is a pleasant place to reside. It has comfortable lounges upstairs and downstairs and a well-stocked, sheltered garden. Work on a new annexe extension is shortly to be completed and will provide six extra rooms and an airy sunroom. The home aims to provide a safe, friendly environment where independence is encouraged. Faye is the General Manager who sets high standards and ensures things run smoothly. The residents cause exceptions to this by wandering off, tripping up or ringing 999 to report non-existent emergencies. There is never a dull moment in a place where you would expect nothing much to happen. Faye promotes a family type atmosphere, but with any group of people there will be inevitable disagreements and squabbles to be refereed, to maintain the status quo. She shares her time between the portfolio of homes she manages. Her right-hand woman is Alison Summers, Registered General Nurse, responsible for the health and wellbeing, medicating and patching up of twenty two residents, some of whom require a lot of nursing care and all who need a bit of love. When Alison attended her job interview Faye knew instantly that she would fit in and be committed to delivering the level of care required. Her lovely smiling face, enthusiasm for caring for the elderly and sense of humour came shining through. Faye was so happy when Alison accepted the job offer. That was three years ago, some staff have left, others have just arrived and it's Alison's job to keep them all on board with adhering to procedures and doing the right thing.

Faye and Alison mostly have a good working relationship but there have been some disagreements over matters of cost. Faye tries to do everything as economically as possible but when it comes to comfort and niceties Alison won't cut corners and will hold out for the best for her patients. This causes some friction between but they always manage to agree, or compromise in the end.

The most established residents who reside on the first floor are Bella, Ethel, Maude and Ada. Wilfred and Bernard have adjacent rooms on the second floor which also has a dining room where they all like to eat together. They always sit in exactly the same position and woe betide anyone who tries to intercept and change their rituals. Bernard has lived at Mount Pleasant View for five years and has seen lots of change, some of which he remembers, and the rest he sadly does not. In the latter years of his working life he helped to manage and tend the 12 acres of land that is The Alnwick Gardens, owned by the Duchess of Northumberland. He has a wealth of experience and knowledge of plants and especially loved working in the Japanese cherry orchard. He cannot stop dead-heading and pruning as it is an embedded behaviour. Jim, the employed gardener at Mount Pleasant View likes to see the beneficial effects that the garden provides everyone and encourages Bernard to potter there. With a permanent stoop now, Bernard jokes that he is shrinking. Once he stood six feet two inches tall but is far shorter than that. Whether this is due to years of bending or disc degeneration and the ageing process no-one can say for sure. His gnarled hands still tend the plants, it's a life-long pleasure which keeps on giving.

All of the residents have a little emblem on the door to their room that depicts something they like or that is representative of them. A tile slotted into a little wooden frame on room number 16, Bernard's room, displays a picture of a watering can and a pitch fork. This was at his own suggestion but he does wonder how this is all that defines him now, as he once had a beautiful wife, Emmeline who was his world. She captured his heart and walked life's bittersweet journey by his side, no longer with him now, not at least in the physical sense.

Wilfred and Bernard may not have otherwise forged a friendship but for being holed up in the same residential home together. They exchange a bit of banter and whilst playing chess, things can turn into heated disagreement. As no one else understands the rules they ought to do the gentlemanly thing, agree to disagree. Wilfred has been known to say, "If I agreed with you, we would both be wrong". Wilfred's door tile is not chess related; if so he would choose the most important chess piece, the king. However, it's the badge of the Royal Air Force, the eagle volant encircled by the Latin phrase 'Per Ardua Ad Astra, *through adversity to the stars.* As a flight lieutenant, once in charge of a regiment, his only responsibility now is to himself, which is why he always fights a hard battle to achieve 'checkmate'.

The door of room 5 bears the picture of some dancing shoes. Bella knew all of the moves, back in the day. Her cha-cha-cha was both stylish and staccato and when she danced with Albert all eyes were upon them. Like Fred and Ginger they stole the dance floor with their foxtrot and quickstep. They fell for each other and danced their way through life with an enduring love. These days Bella can only take a few steps, unassisted. Now reliant on a walking aid since fracturing her hip she loathes being trapped inside this aged body. Sometimes she forgets and thinks she is young again. Today she is crying in her room. She is wondering where her mother is, and can't remember when anyone last visited. It's one of her bad days, of mixed-up thoughts and ideas that leave her anxious and confused. Her short-term memory is deteriorating yet she can recall with clarity the events of years ago. She is feeling lonely and frustrated.

Ethel closes the door to her room, number 9, stopping for a second to blow a kiss to her all-time favourite actor and screen icon Sean Connery, depicted there. She often spends her afternoons watching films on DVD. Ethel also loves the old musicals and can often be heard singing along with Doris Day to the sounds of Calamity Jane and Annie Get your Gun. Ethel makes her way along the corridor, she is about to pass Bella's room until she hears crying noises. Instead she pops her head around the door to investigate.

"What's up, love?" she asks sympathetically. Through gappy teeth Bella says, " I don't know what to do, I lost my glasses, I don't know what time it is or if I've had breakfast," Bella is fidgeting and distressed. Her red, watery eyes look troubled and distant.

"It's twelve thirty, time for lunch! Are you hungry, Bella?"

"I'm not sure...if... I am....but I'm sick of sitting here," she stated, shaking her head hopelessly.

Ethel replied, "Your glasses are on your head, and don't forget your teeth are in that jar, come and eat. A bit of lunch will make you feel better. I've seen the menu and its chocolate cake today!"

Bernard notices it's 12:30. He is finding the crossword difficult today, not helped by the small print and his worsening cataracts. He is awaiting surgery for their removal and in the meanwhile he must create the optimum conditions to maximise his vision. He is especially frustrated that he can't think of an answer to 10 across, 11 letters, parapet or molding. The sun has been brightly streaming in all morning so he opens the window to let some cool air in. He folds up the newspaper and places it on the window sill, along with a clutter of items. He is feeling hungry and makes his way to the dining room.

They all take their seats at a large round table with six place settings. Only four of them are gathered around for lunch today as Maude has an out-patient appointment and Ada is off to the podiatrist.

"Hello ladies, I wonder what type of cabbage soup it is today?" asks Wilfred with a wink. He actually asks this every day, so no one bothers to answer. He is following true form. "When I was in hospital the soup tasted the same every day, but it was a different colour," he added. "It had hard bits floating in it, dried, they were, and it was watery, must have been powdered soup, not freshly made".

"Don't be mean about Mrs B's cooking, she does a good job. I like her carrot soup the best. Sweet potato is nice too, never had that when we were young. Ordinary potato was all you got if you were lucky, good old King Eddies mashed with a bit of milk. Now it's all 'Maris Piper', Charlotte and butternut squash" said Ethel.

"Butternut squash isn't potato though, it's pumpkin, it's what the Yanks eat. Still makes a nice soup though," adds Bernard. "Did you know, you shouldn't eat green potatoes? Means they've had too much light and they've produced toxins. Messes with your bowels like something rotten, tummy cramps and diarrhoea, rushing to the toilet, at least it means that you can lay off the laxatives though ..."

"What sort of soup do you like, Bella? asks Wilfred, twiddling his grey moustache and trying to steer away from the subject of bowels, always a popular topic of discussion.

"Well, split pea, lentil and ham I think. I used to make it with dumplings, it was so thick you could stand your spoon up in it. We never went hungry," adds Bella. "Is Albert joining us today, I've missed him. Why hasn't he been?" Ethel, Bernard and Wilfred exchange glances because no one wants to remind Bella that Albert is no longer alive. The news would be received as if the event had happened afresh, even though he died some 10 years ago.

Not wishing to upset Bella again with the brutal truth they all fell silent, their thoughts returning to the more pleasurable matter of food.

"Here's the soup. Ohh it's leek and potato! Do we usually have this on a Tuesday? asks Bernard.

"No, that's because it's Wednesday" corrected Maurice.

"Well, I must've been reading yesterday's paper, thinking it was todays. This soup hasn't got much flavour, can you pass the salt and pepper over?" Bernard irritatingly scrapes every last speck of soup from the sides of the rough glazed bowl, reluctantly relinquishing it to Sally, the carer on serving duty.

"Sausage, gravy and mash, ahh, here it is", declares Bernard, licking his lips. Bella picks up her adapted knife and fork. Sometimes she needs help to cut up her food as her arthritic hands are painfully distorted. First, she tries the creamy mash and onion gravy.

Maurice decides it's time for a joke about sausages. "What about this one? Man walks into a library and says to the receptionist, two sausages please. The receptionist says, I'm sorry, this is a library, sir. The man lowers his voice and whispers, sorry, two sausages please." Bella has just placed a piece of sausage in her mouth and in this lucid moment starts to laugh at the joke. She sharply inhales just at the wrong moment. The piece of meat fires to the back of her throat as if expertly shot from a catapult, on a direct course for her windpipe.

"I have fond memories of the sausage factory, it was the best of times, it was the wurst of times," Maurice continues. "What about the German who……" and he breaks off mid-sentence.

Bella is suddenly clutching, grasping at her throat in terror, her eyes are wild and she cannot speak. In fact, she cannot breathe, cough or do anything at all. The sausage is lodged there, obstructing her airway. Her arms were flailing around and only a slight squeak of a stridor could be heard.

"Get Alison, help, help!" shouts Ethel desperately. "Bella is choking!!"

Sally (who cleared the soup bowls) has never dealt with an emergency. Despite her recent first aid training session she can't recall what to do, but she does remember Alison telling her she must pull the emergency cord. In her panic and inability to do anything more constructive, she manages to raise the alarm.

In the office downstairs, Alison is writing reports and making sure her documentation is updated. She sees the Zone 4 light flashing high up on the wall and hears the continuous emergency buzzer. As first responder she sprints upstairs, her heart rate increasing as she tries to anticipate what is happening. She immediately claps eyes on Bella whose lips are blue, her eyes rolling back. Ethel doesn't need to tell Alison that Bella can't breathe. Alison rushes behind Bella who is just beginning to slump forward, places her arms around her waist and clenches her fist. Then grasping hold of her other fist she performs some abdominal thrusts and prays that the Heimlich manoeuvre will work. On the sixth attempt the obstruction is dislodged. A chunk of sausage ejects from Bella's throat; the meaty missile hurtles two metres through the air before bouncing off the linoleum. Gasping greedily for breath, Bella has been snatched back from the arms of death. The shocked and silent spectators break into a round of applause in appreciation of the heroic act. Alison's face is bright red with exertion, her auburn fringe sweatily stuck to her forehead. "Is an ambulance on its way? Bella needs some oxygen and will have to be checked over at the hospital, that was very traumatic!" She exclaimed.

'Anyone for chocolate cake?" Bernard enquires. "I wouldn't mind polishing off that spare piece if it's going to waste".

Faye and Alison met up a couple of hours later. A 'critical incident debrief' was necessary to discuss how Bella had almost fatally choked. They decided that sausage could no longer feature on the menu as it had proven far too risky.

"I must say, extremely well done, thank goodness that you managed the crisis so efficiently! It would have been tragic to lose Bella that way, not to mention the bad press, involvement of the coroner and all the general upset for our residents," remarked Faye.

"That's the one and only time I've had to do that, I can't tell you how relieved I was to see that piece of sausage shooting back out. Poor Bella was so frightened. There was nothing wrong with her ability to swallow, you know, it was just one of those things." Alison shakes her head whilst reflecting on the awful drama.

"Alison, I've heard that some of the other managers on our patch are preparing for unannounced visits from the Care Quality Commission. I've just received a letter of notification from them; they could come to inspect us at any time. I think we need to make sure all of our risk assessments are up to date, with supporting documentation in case we are asked to produce evidence around our compliance with our policies".

"Ohhh no, not the CQC," groaned Alison, putting her head despairingly in her hands. "There's never a good time for that! What about staff training records, storage and administration of pharmacy drugs, infection control standards....the list is endless! Suddenly my day has become even worse, if that's at all possible!"

"Well I think we need to review what we have, and also what we don't have. That way, we put things in place before *they* spot what's missing. I'm anxious that we maintain our 'good' star rating at all costs.

I'm going to check our fire safety procedures, evacuation plan, make sure the fire exits are all accessible and kept clear. I don't think there should be any issues, but you never know. You just can't be too careful!" Faye looks down at her purple varnished nail extensions, inspecting the chipped surface. With her long chestnut hair falling over her shoulders and fluttery eyelashes she looks more like a model than a home manager. "I'd better get these off, and can you check up on everyone else, please? Nail polish is an infection risk. And ask the girls if they are washing their hands as often as they should."

"What about Ben and Steve, care assistants, don't forget the importance of equality and diversity, it's something else to add to your list," warned Alison, her finger wagging and her eyes rolling skywards. "Oh, and there's information governance as well!"

"Got it", says Faye, then adds, "Those old dining chairs you keep telling me about, I think we should replace the split seats after all. And *we* need to ask Edgar to clean out the canary cage more often and produce a cleaning checklist".

Alison didn't know whether to laugh or cry.

In room 16 the sun's strong rays have been beaming in over the course of the afternoon. As a boy scout Bernard must surely have tried to burn leaves or paper with a magnifying glass. However, it was the last thing on his mind when he placed it in close proximity to his newspaper on the window sill. Off he went for lunch with thoughts only of quashing his hunger pangs. The thermal rays spread over the surface of the lens, intensifying in a single area. A tiny wisp of smoke spiralled from the focal point on the newspaper which now bore a brown, charred hole, taking out 10 across, 2 down and 7 across. The window sill was smouldering and random sparks leapt up onto the curtains.

In the lounge, Ethel was waiting on one number for a line; the prize money was a mere five pounds but she was still excited at the prospect of winning. Man alive, number 5, Heaven's gate 78, staying alive 85, Doctor's orders number 9. "BINGO," shouts Ethel, just as the fire alarm's piercing tone sounded.

"That's the fire alarm, is it a test? What day is it? It's not Friday, and it's not 11:00. Has someone burnt the toast?" asks Wilfred, trying to reason this as the fire safety doors abruptly clunk shut. Some of the carers rush out of the room to see what's happening, some others rush back in against them and shout, "Fire on the second floor. We must evacuate. No-one must use the lift, everyone must go outside to the meeting point and remain there until told otherwise. More staff are coming to assist those of you who need help.

"What the heck? Says Ethel, "Where's me five pounds?"

"Never mind that, let's go or we will all be toast," states Bernard." Second floor? Hope it's not in my room", he mused. Now the emergency sirens can be heard, becoming louder and louder until the fire engine screeches to a halt in the car park. Several firefighters jump down, all in full safety kit, and they address Faye as they enter the home. "Room 16 is on fire and there's smoke in the corridor, second floor", she briefs them. "We don't know how it started."

The residents form a Zimmer frame evacuation procession and wait obediently at the meeting point until the fire is successfully extinguished. Bernard heard that his room is at the epicentre of the drama. Large tears roll off his nose and drip on the ground. Like a small child awaiting reprimand, he is dreading the consequences. Will he be able to stay at Mount Pleasant, and if not, where will he end up? Ohh no, God no, his photograph of Emmeline...he couldn't bear for it to be destroyed.

Eventually, when it was deemed safe to do so, they were all allowed to go back in. Some were jostling to be first to find out what had caused the fire, and to see the damage. The rest shuffled in, or were wheeled in, all wrinkling their noses at the acrid smoke smell lingering in the air.

Bernard's room was completely out of bounds, taped off whilst a full investigation into the cause of the fire was launched. Photographs were taken to record the damage of the charred scene. Lots of Bernard's personal effects were destroyed: his slipper soles reduced to rubbery blobs, his gardener's award like a melted wax Oscar.

At least the most important possession has not perished. With her head in a thrown back pose, Emmeline, captured for all time in sepia, is the only one who is laughing at the plight of the devastated room. Bernard is temporarily relocated to the overnight guest room and his magnifying glass has been confiscated. Just a few days later, before the dust had time to settle, so to speak, three official looking figures walked up the path to the home. Clutching files and clip boards and sporting the purple identity lanyards of the CQC, they looked like they meant business. They reported to the receptionist, waiting to be introduced to the person in charge. News of their presence had spread to the higher floor within seconds of their arrival.

In the kitchen they noted the absence of daily fridge temperature recordings and they observed Mrs Bentham, the cook, licking a spoon. There were some food storage issues but the area was generally clean and tidy. Moving on to the dining room they watched the food being served and requested to sample everything on the menu. They commented to each other on the attentive servers, how they helped to butter toast, provide condiments, and that hand wipes were available for all. The split seat coverings were conveniently concealed by the bottoms that were sitting upon them. Then they divided up, one was to continue with the environmental checks and the others would interview the residents and staff. In the lounge, Edgar had just let Tweety Pie the yellow canary out of his cage. The little bird was delighted at this gesture of temporary freedom and flew around the room, pecking at the wallpaper seam. Into the room came the inspector who smiled at Edgar and introduced herself. She asked him how long he had lived there and what he liked, or didn't so much like, about the facilities. Edgar launched into full flow and said he loved it here, the staff were so caring and would get him anything he needed. Tweety Pie swooped down and landed on the lady's bun, fastened tightly on her head. He stamped his little feet up and down on her hair, pecking and pulling out some strands, to fashion a nest.

When he pooped on her shoulder she shrieked and ran from the room. Her colleague wanted to ask Wilfred about his experiences of living at Mount Pleasant so he told her about the comfortable pillows. "We've got new corduroy pillows, he explained, "They're making headlines everywhere!" It took a few seconds for her to laugh and say, "Ohh yes, that's very good, I get it!"

No-one could possibly gauge how the inspection had gone. When they put their stories together they worried that an improvement notice might be served. However, when Faye received the report ten days later she was delighted to have maintained the overall rating of 'good'. Despite the choking incident, the fire and the canary misdemeanour it was such a positive outcome.

Jim the gardener was asked to put out the red, white and blue bunting. They threw a celebratory party with egg and cress sandwiches and cakes, washed down with Shloer. Ethel sang 'Whatever Will Be, Will Be' and 'White Cliffs of Dover' in her thready-though-tuneful voice. Everyone had a happy day. If you think you would like to live at Mount Pleasant View, please contact Faye. You will be pleased to hear there are some rooms still available in the newly opened extension.

Soul Home

"Douglas is such a bright boy, sometimes I have to remind myself that he is barely four years old", remarked Mrs Peters, his nursery school teacher. "He's obsessed with birds and can name a great variety of species!"
"Mrs Peters," said Douglas, "I know puffins, kittiwakes and guillemots and can show you in my book!" he smilingly stated.
"Yes, you're really good at remembering them all. Could you go and play for a few minutes while I talk to your Mum, please?"
"Ok," he replied, crouching down to tie his shoelace.
"Mrs Chalmers, Douglas is displaying cognitive abilities, creativity and behavioural habits at a higher level than most other children of his age" she explained. "He may be a 'gifted child' which is a wonderful thing, though not without its challenges!"
Evelyn Chalmers is smiling and nodding at the suggestion, for this is something she has considered.

Mrs Peters further explained, "Gifted children may display highly artistic or musical abilities. We can hold off on any formal assessment until Douglas is age 5 to 6 as there are very few specialist pre-school programmes.

"Everyone thinks their child is special, but I do think there is something...different...unusual.. about Douglas and I'm glad that you see it too," remarked Mrs Chalmers. "He has a vivid imagination and is always making up stories. I really don't know where his ideas come from!"

"Intelligent children are very sensitive to their environment and tend to daydream. They express themselves through play; Douglas is simply trying to engage and interact with the world around him".

Mrs Chalmers began, "Yes, but sometimes he talks about people and places that he couldn't possibly have knowledge of. He sings sea shanties that I've never heard! When I was putting him to bed he told me he missed Archie. He doesn't know anyone of that name, so naturally I was puzzled, and asked the question. He said that Archie was his *best f*riend *from the last time, when he was small.* Well, that was also a strange thing to say. He told me he used to live in Scotland! I have to say that a shiver went right through me! I said, "Douglas, now how can that be, we have always lived in Northumberland", and he replied, *well you have, Mummy, but you don't know where I used to be.* I ruffled his hair and kissed him goodnight. He made me feel uneasy. Have you heard of anything like this before? *Is it normal*?" she asked.

"It's very common for children to talk of imaginary friends. Douglas is very bright and expressive. Please don't worry about it; we will continue to monitor things for the moment and talk again soon. Now, I'm sure that our forthcoming trip to Amble for the puffin cruise will give us all something to look forward to. The trip is on 20th July, just before we break up, so I will be asking for payment and some volunteers to join us. The boat heads out to Coquet Island about a mile off shore and I'm hoping the children will see lots of marine wildlife".

Mrs Chalmers replied, "I can't come along for the trip as I'm working that day. I'm sure Douglas will enjoy it and be in safe hands. Mrs Peters, can I ask, have you ever heard Douglas speaking with a Scottish accent?"

The day of the trip arrived and the weather was sunny. Mrs Peters, fourteen children and four assistants queued up on the Amble dock and waited for the Beryl Tollemache, a decommissioned RNLI boat, to return from the island. The little ones jumped up and down excitedly, their assorted coats formed a rainbow of colour along the jetty. Douglas was not engaging with anyone. He was preoccupied with the knotted ropes lying on the slipway. Bowline, reef, clove hitch, he was able to identify each one. He was unusually sullen and silent. As he looked out to where the River Coquet's flood water meets the North sea, tears coursed down his face. He felt wholly unsettled at the sight of the breaking waves. When it was time to board the boat he flatly refused. Mrs Peters stooped down to his level and said, "Come on Douglas, take my hand and we will get on the boat together. I think you will be the first to see a puffin, and there is a prize!"

His little body stiffened and he held his breath until he turned blue. Mrs Peters decided she would pick him up and carry him on board but he started screaming, "No, no, I don't want to, I'm not getting ON THAT BOAT!"

"But Douglas, this boat was used to rescue people and is perfectly safe. C'mon, you don't want to miss everything do you?" said Mrs Peter's in her soft, persuasive voice.

Douglas took a deep breath and shouted, "Haud yer wheesht, I'll give ye a skelpit lug!" as he lashed out, narrowly missing Mrs Peter's face.

Douglas most definitely would not get on board so instead was taken to the cafe by one of the assistants. Mrs Peters had never seen Douglas behave so outlandishly and she certainly couldn't account for his bizarre, Scottish accent. She tried hard to make sure the rest of the children had fun, but the incident hung over the day like a black cloud. Douglas had told her to 'shut up or he was going to bash her on the ear'.

In the northern Scottish isle of Shetland, the 20th July 1881 dawned clear, with a pleasant breeze. The short summers are typically cool and strong winds in the preceding days kept the boats in port. Haaf fishing has always been an important part of the islands' economy and the sixareen (six oared) crews were under constant pressure to fish for their livelihood. Fearing the burden of debt, they often took risks at sea, in unpredictable conditions. The men had tarred the traditional boats in preparation of the fifty mile long journey to the fishing grounds. The trip would last three days and they baited and set up their lines to catch herring and ling. The boat carried a square sail for use in sufficient winds though the crew might row for many hours to complete the journey.

Laurence Sandison and Archie Sinclair were best friends. They grew up together and at the age of sixteen were on the verge of manhood. The two were in high spirits due to the break in the weather and the prospect of their fishing trip, ever keen to demonstrate the skills they had been taught by their elders.

Ma Eva watched her son Laurence leave their croft house on his way to meet Archie and the rest of the crew. Her eyes fixed upon him until his form disappeared from view. She knew that each trip was a necessary evil for the exposed boats afforded no protection from the elements. Her anxiety was shared by all the womenfolk whose husbands and sons fished the perilous sea.

"I'll keep da fire burning for ye, 'nd a pot on da stove", she shouted, though her voice could not possibly carry far enough for him to hear. Skipper Williamson was experienced and acquainted with the complex geology of the rugged coastline. He used such landmarks as hilltops and openings between the islets or 'voes' for navigation, in the absence of sophisticated instruments.

The Spindrift set away on a relatively calm sea, though a freak storm was brewing; a fast-moving and rapidly developing depression from Iceland whipped up the gale force winds. The sky blackened, ferocious waves pounded their boat and the rain lashed down. No amount of strength or expertise could save them from the extreme conditions. The crew battled against the elements but the violent forces of nature capsized their boat and dragged them all to a watery grave.

"Archie, Archie, hold on!!" Douglas sat bolt upright, relieved to find he was in bed, in the room that was decorated with a frieze of birds. He recalled the stark, stone walls of his Shetland home and how cold it always was. The warmest room was heated by an open fire nestled in a huge fireplace; such a comforting place of protection. Ma Eva had cherished him then, and mourned his tragic loss. He pictured her, standing in the doorway, waving him goodbye, though neither of them knew it would be for the last time. His body was never returned from the sea, there could be no earth burial but his soul was sentient. The weather, the sea, the screeching birds were exactly the same as he remembered them on that fateful day. How could he board the boat in the knowledge of how things might end?

Evelyn came to his room to comfort him. It had been a stressful day for both of them, especially when she was informed of her son's meltdown. Mrs Peters offered the help of an ex-colleague and friend who has experience in such matters. He was interested to talk to Douglas and include him in his research case studies.

"Douglas, I don't know how to help you with this so we are going to see an expert; a professor who knows about these things. I know that there are things that trouble you and I want to be able to understand."

Dr Bradley Atkinson is a child psychiatrist with a special interest in past life memories. His meeting with Douglas and Evelyn was edifying and he soon became embroiled in the story that Douglas shared of his past life on Shetland. He documented and recorded the interview as he gathered information for the case study. He told them he would carry out some investigations and prepare a report which he would email to them. At the end of the session the doctor shook Douglas's hand, saying it was a pleasure to meet him.

"Thank you and I know you believe it's all true", said Douglas with a knowing smile.

Hello Mrs Chalmers,

It was a pleasure to meet you and Douglas and since our meeting I have certainly been busy!

I made enquiries in order to substantiate some facts about Douglas's past life. The Shetland Family History Society holds a wealth of information on family names and ancestry. They confirmed that Eva Sandison was born in Lerwick in 1840, and that she gave birth to a baby boy in 1865 named Laurence (Sandison). The father was Magnus Sandison, place of birth was also Lerwick, though in 1835. I discovered that he died in traumatic circumstances and wonder if Douglas can elaborate. There was also a death registration for Archibold Sinclair, presumed drowned at sea, circa 20th July 1881, the day of a severe storm which caused the loss of one hundred and five men from a total of seventeen boats. There is no scientific explanation as to how Douglas's experiences match the historical records; his soul is truly connected to the place and event. It may be cathartic for Douglas to visit Shetland to try to find inner peace; certainly this has proven to be a positive experience for the children I have studied. If we were to progress this, it would be sensitively managed, and I would happily give you my professional and financial support. I am prepared to subsidise a trip paid from my research funds if you think that Douglas might benefit from the experience. I look forward to your response.

Dr B Atkinson.

"Douglas, we are going to Shetland so you can show us where you used to live", said Evelyn.

"I'd love that!" he replied. "Isn't it strange that Ma Eva named me Laurence which means 'bright shining one' and you called me Douglas, meaning 'dark waters'... and there's something else! I remembered that my Da,

Magnus, was unloading crates and got crushed between a cargo ship and the quay...that's how he died. Who is he? And where do you think he is he now?"

The Foundling Wheel

It was a simple, rustic place to enter the world, in the fading hours of daylight. The orchard buzzed to the low tune of lazy bees and rhythmic cricket song and there, in the thicket of the lemon grove, Rosina lay. She had carefully chosen this place for the shady privacy it afforded and when the labour pains began she settled onto the bale of straw that would be her birthing bed. It was with fearsome foreboding, for she knew something of the pain she would experience. Child birth had already brought tragedy to the family when both mother and infant had died within days of the event. Now their father was an angry man made bitter with grief, who dragged himself through days that were devoid of purpose. Rosina avoided him, protecting herself from his short fused temper and heartless ways.

Throughout the day Marco brought fresh water and cold compresses for her forehead, supporting and encouraging her through this test of endurance. Finally, the sun's russet glow extinguished as the moment of parturition came and the baby was delivered. "A boy", he said, and Rosina looked into his eyes with the terrible fear that lived inside of her. Taunted by demons, she believed the baby would be deformed and covered in thick black hair, a devil's child. Yet Marco saw only an exquisite infant of perfect form. Knowing that she was troubled by these dark thoughts he uttered, "Corpo perfetto", beautiful body, the words coursed through his smiles and tears.

Rosina stole her one and only look at the baby; the sight of him must remain captured in her heart and mind forever. Marco cut the cord, wrapped the newborn and laid him in a fruit basket lined with muslin. It was time to carry out the rest of their plan and it was better done swiftly and without complication. No one must ever learn the shameful truth.

He took the winding road leading down to the village, carefully mapping every step and carrying the basket with the greatest care. He met no-one on this carefully chosen route that bypassed the distant farmhouses, their presence punctuated only by squares of light. It was rocky and uneven in places but he was unfaltering and sure-footed. The sound of a barking dog cut into the night air but all else was still as he trekked onwards through the olive groves, cypress trees and lavender fields, the aroma ever fresh and pungent. The fragrances enveloped him, wafting and carrying him on his way. Soon he would see the lights of the village, bringing the journey to its sombre conclusion. Approaching the market place he was thankful to see it empty; the folk who jostled and bargained there by day, selling their produce had long since returned to their farmsteads. Only a single horse-led cart clattered through the cobbled street, taking its direction from a lone rider.

Just around the corner the looming tower of the ancient convent dominated the landscape. He had seen inside of the chapel before with its black and white mosaic floor representing the colours of good and evil. A carved statue of Christ with arms outstretched guarded the entrance with grace and stony solemnity. Marco knew that the foundling wheel, 'Culla per la vita' (life cradle) was situated at the side entrance; a hatch on the outside bearing a revolving crib. Here he gently laid the baby and placed a single kiss on his head to mark their bitter parting. He rang the bell, the sound of it so jarring and melancholy, then turned the handle, gently swinging the baby from the outside world to a room of inner sanctuary. Marco began running, never once looking back and the pain of the irreversible act overcame him now.

It was Sister Angelique who responded to the sounding bell and she lifted the baby from the metal cradle and into her arms. In the flickering candlelight she carefully inspected him, studying his perfect little form in wonderment. In keeping with convent tradition as the first nun to attend, she chose to call him Angelo, a derivative of her own name meaning "angel" or "messenger".

Marco made his solitary journey home; he could not suppress his heartache and feelings of remorse. This was the only possible ending and the consequences tore him apart. He would return to Rosina, *his sister and lover* to tell her their child had been safely accepted into the convent. If they should ever be reunited it would be the work of a miracle.

Bridget of Brancepeth

Safely encircled by the great walls of Brancepeth Castle lives a lonely little girl called Bridget. She is playing cheerfully with her dolls and her rocking horse, Remus, though from its very beginning her life was steeped in irreversible sadness. Her mother became ill in the days following childbirth and fell prey to the desecration known as childbed fever. Beyond medical help she slipped away, her untimely death left Bridget to the care of her father, William.

What could William have known about caring for this baby girl? As a Member of Parliament for Durham William spent much of his time on political business in London so he called upon his sister Frances to care for the child. Bridget had an isolated existence, seeking solace in a happier world of play. She developed a lively imagination and engaged in whimsical dialogue with her dolls. The boy doll was her favourite, dressed richly in a blue satin waistcoat and breeches. He wore a linen shirt, lace cravat and silk stockings. His outer layer was a red woolen coat with gold embroidery and shiny buttons. Coiffured human hair was nailed to his wooden head! His leather shoes were fashionably topped with buckles. He was the epitome of a contemporary gentleman. Sometimes he would ask his female doll counterpart, Betsy to walk out to the river with him, admiring her pale painted face and glass eyes before returning to their designated shelf in the nursery.

Bridget explored the castle's long corridors, looking down through the high arched windows at the circular courtyard below, and up at the buttresses, battlements and turrets. Running her hands over the huge stone fireplaces with blackened grates and along the shiny wooded bannisters of the grand staircase she made up little songs that she sang under her breath.

On Sundays they walked to St Brandon's Church for worship. Bridget liked to look at the ornate Gothic carvings whilst listening to Rector Thomas read Bible passages and deliver sermons on how to achieve righteousness. Bridget's Aunt Frances taught her to read, write and sew. She was charitable towards Bridget but her serious disposition did not lend itself to shows of affection or spontaneity. Sometimes they listened to music in the afternoon and during one such time there was talk of a travelling show due to perform in the courtyard of the castle. This became the focus of great excitement and raised many questions about who was coming and what it might be like. Aunt Frances described a scene from memory of jugglers, acrobats and dancers and a troupe who enacted Shakespearean plays. Crowds of people were expected to watch the players perform on the cobbled courtyard, all enjoying themselves, noisy with laughter and gin induced merriment. Bridget asked if she would be able to join in, for she had not seen the likes before. Aunt Frances suggested that she might be able to watch from the window only. This would surely be better than nothing, for it was not the place for a child to be exposed to such goings-on.

As a young woman she was granted a little more freedom, though always with a chaperone. Her father took her to a public fair to listen to music quartets and to watch lively scenes performed by travelling theatre companies. This was a different world to Bridget who absorbed the atmosphere and enjoyed its frivolity. It was here where she was first introduced to Robert Shafto, a politician who moved in similar social circles. He was from a family of merchants but became involved in election campaigning. His Whitworth Hall home could be seen across the River Wear from the highest windows in Brancepeth Castle. Situated on the outskirts of Spennymoor, the close proximity of his residence made them relatively close neighbours. Robert chatted away to them in an animated fashion. He appeared larger than life and oozed both charm and charisma.

Bridget was immediately taken with Robert who cut a dashing figure. He was tall and slim, his striking appearance made so by his flamboyant dress style. His laughing eyes held Bridget's full attention and she was secretly delighted to learn of his forthcoming visit to Brancepeth. Robert planned to see his brother, Rector Thomas to update him on the most recent trip to London and his latest electioneering efforts. In four weeks he would attend the Sunday church service then take lunch afterwards. As the conversation drew to a close he proffered an exaggerated bow to Bridget who fluttered and blushed, and bade him farewell. William sensed that Bridget was distracted for the rest of the day. She had asked him a few casual questions about Robert, she clearly did not follow the plot of the play, or even take much interest in the 'never before seen' Punch and Judy show. As darkness fell, the firework display was not the only thing to light up her eyes that day. Bridget greatly looked forward to Sunday service like she never had before. It brought another opportunity to see Robert who she had thought of all day and dreamed of at night. She fretted and fussed over what to wear, questioning if her Sunday best would be good enough to catch Robert's eye. Her favourite silk mantua gown was the garment of choice; its cream fabric adorned with red flowers and frilled sleeves was a cut above the rest. On meeting her once more Robert doffed his hat in an act of courtesy. They discussed the weather then he told her he was shortly to sail to London, a fairly dangerous enterprise, though preferable to that of a road trip for fear of Highwayman attack. He would come to see her in a few weeks, and she could refer to him by his nickname, Bobby. With each passing day Bridget became more fanciful and infatuated. She documented their meeting in her diary and counted the days to his return. In her chambers she penned the first verse of a ditty,

"Bobby Shafto's Gone to Sea,

With silver buckles on his knee,

He'll come home and marry me,

Bonny Bobby Shafto!"

This is what she truly hoped for and believed, though Bobby's friendly demeanour made him popular with the ladies and he was responsible for a string of broken hearts. In London Bobby mixed business with pleasure, cementing his brief relationship with Anne Duncombe by asking for her hand in marriage. This was a prudent proposal as Anne was an heiress to the richest commoner in England and their alliance would ultimately increase his family's fortunes.

Bridget waited endlessly and pined for Bobby's return. She could not eat or venture outside, such was her depression and despair. She lost weight and developed a pale complexion, her once bright eyes now soulless and unable to tolerate light. She did not know if she was heartbroken or suffering from an illness. Then came the cough, the pain and the blood on her handkerchief, the news that Bobby was betrothed to another. There was simply nothing left to live for as she lay on her deathbed, ravaged by consumption and weakly mouthing the meaningless words,

'He's my love forever more, bonny Bobby Shafto.'

<u>One Way, and Another</u>

Who do you see when you gaze at my portrait? The mysterious part of me is best represented by darkness and blurred edges of what is seen and unseen. This is especially pertinent as, after all of these years, I am still exploring my concept of 'whole self" and the limits of my boundaries.

My tale begins when, as a seven year old boy, I was curiously attracted to my sister's Christmas present of a pale green tutu; I knew even at that tender age that dressing up as Superman could hold nothing for me. I longed to touch the smooth satin bodice and the springy layers of net that flaunted femme attitude. I hastily tried it on and glanced in the mirror which framed me like a snapshot in time. I was both thrilled and confused at the ridiculous sight. If this was normal then why did I feel I was doing something wrong, I wondered.

In my early twenties I discovered The Wig Shop on a covert, cobbled lane in town. Ladies with alopecia were welcomed through the front door and I came to realise that, for some reason, men loitered at an opposing door. I noticed a small sign pinned there that stated, '*By appointment only.*' I rather fancied trying on some wigs so I waited until an assistant saw me and beckoned. "You can come through love, if you wish. There aren't any other customers here at the moment", she said. I glanced over my shoulder as one might do before entering a den of iniquity, which was hardly necessary in the circumstances. I noticed her name badge. "Let's do this, Gloria", I said.

About twenty guillotined mannequin heads stared blankly at me from the wall-to- wall shelving. Long and short hairstyles, blonde and brunette, jet black, no fringe, long fringe, bouncy red curls, Mary Quant bobs, shades of grey and every ombre in-between were on display. "You'll need to sit in a curtained off booth in case any ladies come in", she directed, adding that *she would bring the other items through for me to look at.* Heaven forbid that any female should be unwittingly

exposed to the sight of six feet three inch me in a blonde curly wig, and built like a brick shithouse.
"What size shoe....?" she called from the stockroom.
"Size 12", I replied hesitantly. She rustled through some boxes then placed the killer stilettos in front of me. I had never seen such shoes of pointy pillar box red and I stared at them as if they were alien beings.
"Well, give'em a try, my lovely," she urged and so I felt obliged to hastily whip off my socks. "Strut!" she ordered me. I stuffed my feet into them and tottered across the linoleum like Bambi on ice. With a sudden urge to be dramatic I flicked my fake blonde curls over my shoulder and pouted. I think you could say I needed only a small amount of encouragement to get into character.
"Make up next", she cried as she promptly plastered my beard area with pan stick foundation, blushed and then highlighted my cheekbones. Ruby red lipstick was a perfect match for the shoes. False eyelashes and kohl 'guyliner' completed the look. She transformed me into

a drag version of Farrah Fawcett in under five minutes. I felt bemused and yet strangely liberated!

"How do you feel?" she asked.

"Simply amazing," I replied. "Meet my alter ego...Anneka!"

The eighties marked a new era of ground-breaking music and fashion that paved the way for men like me.

Top of the Pops and Radio One aired Boy George and the 'girl or a boy' debate raged. George's sidekick Peter Robinson was better known as Marilyn and they blurred the gender line at a time when it was rare and unconventional. I adored Vivienne Westwood's punky, unisex style. Cyndi Lauper sang True Colours just for me. I met and fell in love instantly with Josie at the Glastonbury Festival and for a long time we were great together. We plaited flowers into each other's hair and shared clothes that fitted us both. We married in haste. Our symbiotic relationship allowed us to develop our esoteric fashion styles but also, in her case, a propensity to *swing both ways.* This caused the demise of our relationship as I tried to decide which way I was swinging, or indeed, if I was swinging at all. We divorced.

I met Gabriel in the very unusual and precarious circumstance of climbing the Tyne Bridge after too many drinks and a spliff. He talked me down, calling himself my Angel Gabriel. I guess that was so as he did save me that night, but not for the subsequent merry dance he led me on, resulting in me taking an overdose. It was just a silly cry for help but no-one felt sillier than me when I awoke in A&E with the realisation that a nurse had seen my cerise, ribbon trimmed cami-knickers when she removed my wet jeans. I told myself it wouldn't be the first time or the last for either the nurse or me because they feel so much nicer than boxer shorts.

So what are you thinking now as you study my face? I'm certain to have surprised you with the things I have revealed. No doubt you are wondering about my sexuality and my gauche, feminine side. I bet you want to label me as one thing or another, just as I have sought all my life to do so. One thing I have learned is that we don't all fit into boxes and we can fall in and out of love fluidly. We can shape but not necessarily define ourselves. Could I ask you to simply accept me for who I am, for what you do know of me, then maybe I can begin to accept myself?

I've only told you part of my life story, and the reality is, *you don't know the half of it.*

On The Oak King's Watch

Sienna kicked off her shoes and ran through the golden field, bringing her senses back to life. Her hair was the colour of yellowish-brown earth pigment and it was no mistake that her name insinuated its hue. A shimmering ochre haze hung over the crop field and the wind whipped up and carried her through it. The corn rippled and bristled and she adored its texture against her skin, though her feet experienced an incongruous conflict of pleasure and pain. She visualised the earth's energy flowing upwards. Its natural vibration frequency pulsed through her, providing calm and peace. Grounded now, she felt connected to the earth and protected by its positive ionosphere. Like the parting of ocean waves the sheaves leaned and accommodated, opening a pathway as she moved forward and she knew the spirit was present. The Spirit of the Corn was here! She lay down, feeling its enveloping presence all around.

As if bathing in a sea of corn she was invigorated and reawakened. Soon she would prepare the Corn Dolly as she did this time every year, the skill having been passed down to her by her beloved Grandmother. Such a symbol of good luck and fertility must be prepared with attention to detail, and with love. She would finish making it in time for St Johns Eve and it would sit amidst the bonfire in celebration of this harvest and to ensure the success of the one to follow.

Sienna reflected that her recent health issues had passed now. She had been unwell; a disabling condition made her irritable and drained her energy over the last few weeks. She blamed the weather phenomena for producing symptoms such as migraine and generalised weakness. It made her restless and unable to apply herself to any task. Foehn symptoms caused by low pressure and high winds made her ill and were seemingly destructive to her circadian rhythms, though others were quick to dispel the theory. She was aware of some extreme cases where locals had been driven to madness, had embarked on waves of crime and even committed suicide! In these parts the strong North

Easterly Helm wind hits the south west slopes of Cross Fell escarpment, the highest peak of the Pennines. The wind on the leeward side of the mountain has a warm, drying effect on its descent and is a product of this particular landscape and weather conditions. Warning tales of damage to buildings, livestock and vegetation were re-invented at the onset of each Helm wind season. Stories of when Jefferson's barn was battered by the storm and the time when little Eva was picked up and carried along by the wind were stern reminders of the extreme forces of nature. Strongest in the month of May, those who are sensitive to variable barometric pressure would heed the rumours of its impending arrival and dread its coming.

"Keep a watch for dramatic cloud formations, for when lenticular clouds appear, the Helm winds are near!"

The women of the village spent the preceding days foraging for specific flowers and plants. Fennel, lemon verbena and elderflower were picked as was tradition. The feathery leaves of yarrow, historically used in herbal medicine were collected not just for their anti-inflammatory properties but also to ward off witches and evil spirits. Goatsbeard and masterwort were fashioned into a cross to be blessed by a priest, then buried on the eve of St John's day.

Over doors and windows they hung St John's Wort, which since medieval times was used for additional protection. Everything revolved around the seasons and specific dates in the calendar with all measures taken to protect the harvest. According to old customs the crop spirits are contained in those last cuts of corn. The women engaged in lively chatter as they fashioned the corn into the shape of corn dollies, which kept safely over winter would be re-planted with the following year's crops.

The young ladies worked on flower garlands which they placed in the stream; depending on how and where they floated it was claimed they could foretell the future. For anyone finding a rare crinoid fossil in the river, this was considered to be especially lucky, for the star shaped stone was thought to be a fairy coin which would bring good fortune. For someone keen to marry, any sign leading them to a potential beau was eagerly awaited. They prepared perfumed water using the scents of seven plants. Left outside in vessels the dew of night was collected, for bathing in this water would ensure purification for onset of the new season. Community spirit and tradition also brought the men of the village together; they were bonded by the task of gathering branches from fallen trees, thinning hedges and pieces of kindling to make a bonfire. This was known as 'preparing the faggots,' or bundles of brushwood which would then be laid in celebration of the Northumberland 'baal' fires. The bonfire was built and lit in precisely the same spot as every year that had gone before, on 23rd June.

On the windward side of the fields, the smoke passed over the corn which was thought to ward off any evil influences. The bonfire was the most important focus of the Midsummer celebrations, though the village would come alive with an array of associated festivities including feasting, music and fireworks.

Saint John's Eve is a time of celebration before the Feast Day of Saint John the Baptist; it coincides with the longest day of the year and is therefore followed by the shortest night. Its origins are both ancient and mysterious, the Feast marks the beginning of summer, a time of rebirth and renewed life. We are reminded that it is a special time in which to evolve and grow. Under June's Strawberry Moon we find food and nature in abundance and give thanks for the life-giving powers of the sun.

The jaunty notes from a fiddle were heard in the street, soon to be joined by those of penny whistles and the Northumbrian pipes. Then it was time for the dancing to begin and the folks came from their homes to join the celebration. A torch bearer led a procession down to the bonfire, using its flame to light it once the last of the daylight faded. As the dry wood took hold the flames rose higher and higher, illuminating the whole village from far across the valley. The children made a ring around the bonfire, holding hands to represent a circle of life within the universe and eternity. They danced around the fire until such a time that the young men dangerously demonstrated their prowess by jumping through the embers. They made their wishes for personal health, or wealth and to be protected by Mother Nature. It was a promise for the Summer that lay ahead, and if there had been drought they wished for rain. A large cauldron of bread soaked in milk, infused with spices and sugar cooked slowly in the embers of the bonfire then its contents were shared among the crowd in an act of unity. It was a time of great togetherness and peace.

From his lofty position up in the very tallest trees, the Oak King watches over. Reborn at Mabon and crowned with oak leaves and acorns he is resplendently green. At the pinnacle of his strength during the warm days of summer he represents all that is earthy and supportive of new life. Mabon is the midpoint between the

Summer and Winter Solstices when the hours of sunlight and night are equal. When he takes the crown early in the year, the days are long, the crops are tall and new life enters the world. He will steadily rise to full power by the Summer Solstice before being weakened and then defeated by the Holly King in Autumn. He reflects on the seasonal cycles of the year, of solar light and dark, and of crop renewal and growth before going to battle once again with his rival, the Holly King. Autumn and Winter belong to him. His ascension takes place at the year's end when crops do not grow and many living things perish in the cold. Tradition maintains that the Kings fight for the throne at the onset of the Equinoxes and battle ensues again as summer gives way to winter. It is a perpetual battle for dominance through the waxing and waning of the yearly cycles of the Earth.

The Oak King was soon to witness some events that he could neither influence or change during this half year reign, for even he could not harness or overpower the forces of nature. He would simply have to watch and wait for events to unfold.

It was as if Silas Shaftoe had rolled into the village along with the unnatural looking clouds. He was known to no-one in these parts. His black eyes studied the flying saucer and ragged rotor clouds that hung ominously under the mountain crests. He pulled his hat down over his ears, pulled up his cowl collar higher to his neck. In his hand he held a long spear with which he prodded the ground as he walked across the moorland. He noticed that the cows wandered restlessly, swishing their tales and acting skittishly and the air prickled with high electric charge. He continued along this well-trodden path, secure in the knowledge that he would soon reach the thick walled pele tower, his shelter, for he was merely passing through. He would stay long enough to see the effects of the weather at this very unnatural time and then move on. The storm was coming. It was going to be a perfect storm.

Sir Cecil Walton, wealthy property and land owner resides at nearby Eden Hall. He is a real life 'Biggles,' representative of a British hero who is both gentlemanly and eccentric. He is retired now with a penchant for expensive gadgets and hobbies, especially those associated with aerodynamics. His fascination dates back to an early encounter with a Bleriot monoplane which made a bungled landing on his school cricket ground. Now he is the owner of a small aircraft which he regularly flies, to the disdain of his family. However, he is unstoppable and seemingly invincible, in the wake of a few emergency landings in the aircraft which he affectionately refers to as 'my flying coffin'.

Sir Cecil is not superstitious, though he has heard stories of Cross Fell and its connections with evil. He read that in ancient times it was known as Fiends Fell, believed to be haunted by evil spirits and was subsequently blessed by an Archbishop. It is certainly an inhospitable place for much of the year, retaining snow cover into the month of May and even as late as July. Known for its dense fog and a particular shrieking noise of the Helm wind, the mountain still held for him an inexplicable allure. Fancying a little jaunt he stuck his head out of the window and was pleased to see that it was a good clear day. True, that the pressure on his barometer in the hall had fallen a little and though he was intelligent enough to study the data of rainfall, temperature, wind speed and humidity, he simply didn't bother himself to.

Dressed in his flying gear, googles and all he shouted to his wife, "Just taking the flying coffin for a short blast dear, TTFN..." And in case she wasn't sure of the abbreviated meaning, despite having heard him use it hundreds of times before, he added, "Ta Ta For Now!" before closing the front door behind him. With a spring in his step he headed for the airstrip. The take-off was smooth and visibility was good. He reflected on how lucky he was to be able to take such trips independently and to be able to view his estate from above. Climbing higher and gaining a speed of twenty-five knots now he was unexpectedly jostled on hitting a patch of turbulence. The light breeze rapidly whipped up into a fresh gale, catching him in a vertical current which flipped the aircraft, then sandwiched it between airstreams. Completely surrounded by whirling grey mist, Sir Cecil battled with the controls and shouted out every expletive he ever heard of. Beads of sweat rolled down his face and his hands shook. Now in a zone of violent gustiness the unique sound of the Helm wind screamed at him and all around him.

From the ground the bar of cylindrical clouds looked dramatic, like dark flying saucers they were a menacing sight, as if fore warning of impending doom. And that is precisely how Sir Cecil felt, as if his minutes were suddenly numbered and all of his life flashed before him. He had to hold on tight, to keep flying straight through these treacherous conditions until he emerged on the other side. He knew full well that the fuselage could break up mid-air. He had to employ every bit of skill and technical knowledge he could muster if he was to survive this. He cursed himself, "You're a stupid old fool for not checking the forecast, well you're going to have to get yourself back down somehow. Hope for the best, prepare for the worst!" Everything juddered, rolled and oscillated yet his journey persisted through the thick cloud cover. At last the air began to clear and he could see ahead again, though he still battled through the turbulence. Taking it very carefully he slowly began his descent, flipping this way and that like rubbish blown on the breeze. With gritted teeth he braced himself as the ground rose up below him. He could do this! The aircraft smacked onto the ground and screeched to a death-defying halt, bumping along until at last spluttering to a stop. Sir Cecil was not a religious man but he did thank God, Mary, The Baby Jesus as well as his lucky stars that he was alive. He had survived on a wing and a prayer and decided from this day onwards he would become the best version of himself. He was going to live each day as if it were his last; he would become a philanthropist, a pillar of the community and donate to charity. Every single extra day that he was granted on this planet would be a precious gift indeed. Just then he caught a glance of a solitary figure walking close by.

"Hello, hello, I survived, I'm not dead, ha ha!" Sir Cecil he shouted euphorically from the cockpit. The figure did not respond in any way but silently continued on his way. Silas had witnessed it all, and a very interesting show it had been. Sir Cecil thought it strange that there was no interaction between them, considering for a moment that he was perhaps not alive. Just as quickly as the clouds had dispersed, the figure faded from view.

Sir Cecil questioned what he had seen in his heightened state but did not ruminate upon it. "Bugger!" he said aloud, I'm miles from home. I wonder how I shall get back?" Then tapping the cockpit deck he gave grateful thanks to his flying coffin for returning them to terra firma.

The wind gained momentum as it rolled over the pastures, plucking the tops of the tallest trees and bending them. The birds sang less and the bees flew to their hives. The cows seemed strangely flustered. They wandered restlessly then clumped together, vying for cover under the thick shrubbery. Lester Robson was a rookie farm hand, still learning the ways of the countryside though he too could sense the change in the air. Now that May had arrived there was plenty of work to do in the fields for it was time to harvest the cabbage and broad beans. The work would begin this afternoon and he was taking the utility tractor out to assist with the harvesting process. It was hard work and he wasn't feeling his best today, he was plagued with a headache which would not shift and the static in the air irritated his nerve endings. It was if his internal barometer sensed the pressure change but he must get on with his work, at least get started ahead of the impending poor weather. As he started out across the field the watery sun disappeared behind the clouds and would not be visible again for the next few days.

The cows huffed and snorted, they walked in a circle which was a bizarre sight, never seen before. A lone figure walked quietly through the furrows and as he drew closer to the cattle their behaviour became increasingly erratic. They stamped their hooves and tossed their heads; then whipped up into a state of frenzy they charged straight at the stranger.

Lester was driving the tractor and even above the engine noise could hear that something was amiss. He turned around to see what was happening. The cows began charging towards him and in a split second he hit a boulder, causing the tractor to become unstable and overturn. Lester was hurled to the ground and became trapped between the tractor and its unhooked trailer. The cows stood rooted to the spot, as if jolted back to normal by this sudden occurrence. Lester lay crumpled and bleeding, he had excruciating pain in his chest and was unable to move.

Silas had witnessed it all, and in his confused state Lester noticed him standing there and looking on. Faintly he cried out to the stranger, "Help, please help, don't leave me!" His plea was ignored and Silas walked on by, sure footed and not even turning to look back. He wasn't able to help even if he had wished to. He had no conscience and his very soul was fragmented by trauma and the conflict of war. His dark figure marched onwards, seemingly unaffected by the sight of a young man in extremis. Lester stopped crying out, reserving every ounce of strength with which to remain conscious.

At the homestead farmer John Crozier looked at his watch. Time was getting on and he wondered why Lester had not returned. An inexplicable feeling washed over him. Something was wrong and he must go and investigate. The lad still had much to learn but John had invested a lot of effort in him and now found him a great help. Running across the fields he saw the tractor lying on its side and shouted, "Lester, hold on, I'm coming to you." As he drew nearer it appeared there were no signs of life. John shook him by the shoulder, "Lester, open your eyes, look at me. You are going to be ok!"

And Lester did open his eyes with just the tiniest flicker and he trusted John enough to know that he would pull him through this.

The months passed by and the rule of the Holly King completed another cycle. The Oak King reigned again, resplendently green and with foliage in abundance.

The British Meteorological Society became increasingly interested in the Helm winds. This professional society for weather and climate, dedicated to advancing science decided to send some learned members to the village. They journeyed from their base in Reading to the North of England on a special fact-finding mission.

They wished to study any local data relating to barometric pressures, humidity and wind speed, and to interview the villagers on a range of matters. Their findings were to be published in an academic journal in order to increase understanding and to raise awareness of the Helm wind phenomena.

A large sign was pinned up in the church hall to inform of the planned visit. Interested parties were invited along to share their stories of weather damage, associated health issues or anecdotal stories. Excitement rippled through the village as folk were keen to be involved and to put their part of the world 'on the map.' Sienna and Lester met here and chatted to one another, surprised to discover they had experienced similar headache and fatigue symptoms which they wished to discuss with the experts. Foehn effect was at the top of everyone's agenda. They learned more about the windstorms that bring droughts and exacerbate forest fires. The foehn winds were first studied in the Alpine regions where they melted the snow, causing avalanche and flash floods. Such winds affect other countries too; known as 'chinook' in the North America Rockies, Ghibli in Libya and Zonda in the Andes of Argentina, they are responsible for a range of climatic changes.

"I've never met anyone who feels the same as me when the Helm wind blows," Lester declared.

"It's the same for me", Sienna replied, "I thought I was going mad!"

"Maybe we are both a little bit crazy," he said, "but in a good way!" They chattered easily, their conversation flowed and Lester described what had happened on the day of his accident.

"I broke a few ribs and ended up having part of my lung removed, I was in agony for weeks. My femur was shattered, hence I'm still wearing this caliper.... I knew I shouldn't be depressed, more like I should be thankful for being alive, but it was just hard to bear," he sadly disclosed.

"What a dreadful thing to happen, I had far less cause to feel sorry for myself," Sienna reflected.

Sir Cecil came to share what had happened to him. "Hello dear chaps, he said, slapping the backs of the men from the Met office as if they were old friends.

"That Helm wind nearly took the flying coffin and I out!" he told them. "The weather conditions changed just like that", snapping his fingers in demonstration. The interviewers looked most puzzled, and on noticing their expressions he added, "It's my nickname for my light aircraft!" He sat down and began to recount his story in a very animated fashion full of arm waving and sound effects.

Silas Shaftoe has to keep on moving, roaming the moors on foot. There is no rest for him and no pleasure to be found in his lonely existence. This is his penance for being a cruel and heartless raider across the Anglo-Scottish border. Murder, rape and pillage, he had committed them all. He was responsible for terrorising innocent villagers, forcing them from their homes and stealing their cattle. He rustled the livestock, took prisoners for ransom with no regard for their nationality and burned their crops. His soul is trapped and cannot pass into the higher realms. If he is unable to repent, it is his fate to always remain a Border Reiver.

Lester and Sienna felt fortunate to have met in the unusual yet serendipitous circumstances which had brought them together.

"Next St John's Eve my leg will be stronger. I will run through the embers again and make my wishes for the coming year. Will you be there? I mean, might you join me in the Solstice celebrations?"

"I love to see the full moon of Saint John's Eve: it's such a special night of new beginnings, yes of course I will be there," Sienna said. "I have already made my wish to the Spirit of the Corn."

The Oak King's reign had been challenging, yet in his green kingdom the fields looked lush, the tall trees were reaching for the light and another season of growth and nurturing had arrived.

~~~~~~o0o~~~~~
~~~~~~

Printed in Great Britain
by Amazon

19472203R00088